EVERYTHING IN THE GARDEN

EVERYTHING IN THE GARDEN

by

ELIZABETH NORTH

LONDON
VICTOR GOLLANCZ LTD
1978

ISBN 0 575 02380 5

The author acknowledges assistance from the Arts
Council of Great Britain.

Printed in Great Britain by Bristol Typesetting Co. Ltd,
Barton Manor, St. Philips, Bristol

For P. S. J. P. C. S. T.

ONE

BACK IN THE early fifties when you could park quite easily on either side of the wide market street, there was a spacious feeling in the town and individuals were more noticeable.

The main street ran from east to west, and, standing at its centre point outside the town hall by the traffic lights you could look east to hills and countryside and west to hills and countryside, down West Street or along East Street and the small hills were always there in view.

It was an eighteenth-century town of square buildings, well proportioned with sash windows set above shop fronts. Between the shops there were banks and offices, tall buildings facing each other across wide streets. There were solicitors, land agents, estate agents, architects, accountants. From the top windows of these offices you could lean and look to right and left and see the hills at either end.

The country, then, was very near. Streams ran from it down narrow valleys to the north, converging on the town, and joining, becoming what could be called a river and going on into the sea which also was not far. The villages around and up the narrow valleys were quiet places where solicitors and bank managers lived and drove down to work each day. The villages were also full of villagers who came to town on buses, but were fuller still of people who had retired, of ex-army officers, ex-naval officers, a few ex-businessmen, and all these were busy running Parish Councils, Rural District Councils and lived in nice stone houses with sloping lawns to streams and facing each other across the valleys.

In one of the solicitors' offices there was an articled clerk aged twenty-four who would perhaps be taken on to rise to partnership eventually. Or he could go away, and, since he was both energetic and ambitious, many people thought for his sake

7

that he should. He lived with his parents, retired business people from Nottingham, in one of the nicest villages outside the town. And bicycled to work each day.

In an architect's office just along the street was a secretary who also bicycled down each day; she met him at lunch time in a café in between their offices and usually bicycled back with him in the evening. Like him, she often said that she would probably go away. "I might go away one day," she said. But particularly in the summer, when they bicycled home between thick banks of hay-like grass, particularly in June, when yellow butter plant stuck right out in the lanes and brushed their faces and their legs, they said that somehow they both felt quite like staying here.

You could not help but think it was the prettiest place to be. The fields were small, the hedges high, steep banks against which you could sit in the sun, or lie beside. They rode along holding hands because of the sparse traffic. You could hear a tractor or a country bus a mile away and break hands and stand into the banks, bikes well tucked in, and let the vehicle pass. The lanes smelt all the sweeter after the diesel fumes had dispersed above the banks. Willow herb and ragged robin, pink campion and long grass stalks all sprang back and bounced above the tarmacked road.

It was quite romantic and people said how romantic Joan and Richard looked, both very young and unsophisticated and good looking. Their parents on both sides lived in neighbouring villages and got to know each other, but not too well because the pair were very young and no one wants to count their chickens.

He was an only son; his married sister lived in Nottingham, and his mother kept her fingers crossed and hoped he would not go away. It would be a nice life for him as a country solicitor, conveyancing and visiting clients on farms, a nice open-air life for a boy who liked village cricket, county rugby and collecting fossils.

Charmouth, which is on the south-west end of the fossil-bearing belt which crosses England diagonally, was less than ten miles from where they lived.

Because he was alone, he clung to this girl-friend; he saw her as a friend as well as someone sexually desirable; she was also sexually generous which amazed him. She would, for instance, on a warm June day, get off her bike and climb a stile and let him take her clothes off. Not all at once, but gradually, she let him take off more and touch her anywhere he liked. And seemed to like it. Even if she did not like it, she would never say so, but sometimes he would see her looking up at the sky beyond the trees or above the bramble-strands while he was making love to her.

In her office where the sun came through the rather grubby windows, she worked with other girls and seemed quite ordinary. But always let it be known that she was not. She might go away one day and work in London or abroad. All her three older sisters had gone away and it seemed inevitable that she would. Her generation and her social peers all went away to work. They came home at weekends in cars with boy-friends for Hunt Balls and hunting.

So really you were left, if you were Joan, and still, because you quite liked working here and it was pretty and you could not quite make up your mind about where you wanted to go, you were left with farmers' sons and articled clerks like Richard. And she really liked the sex, the bicycling in the summer and the picnics by the streams and being the only one at home.

She worked with other girls and giggled with them in the typing room. But when she went to take dictation every morning, it was from Mr Hodges who was hoping to be a junior partner in the firm and whose office was on the top floor, often sun-filled, dusty, with a heavy desk and filled with pipe smoke.

"I might go away," she said to Mr Hodges the first time she took dictation from him.

"Oh dear," he said. She had good qualifications, a diploma from an expensive boarding secretarial college.

"I might go away some time. I'm only here to cut my teeth."

"I've been away," he said. "In fact I've been away so long that I don't think I'll ever go away again."

"How boring for you," she said in her rather upper-class accent.

"Not at all."

"You're not from round here, are you?"

"No."

"You'll soon get bored."

A*   9

But he was in his thirties, married, settled down and finished. Joan crossed her legs, picked up her spiral notebook and took dictation.

"He's very nice," she said to Richard on the way home, "but rather boring on the whole."

They climbed over a different stile that evening, walked through a field and came into a long narrow wood of tall trees and mossy paths which followed the course of a stream. There were some comfortable love-making places here they'd tried before. But generally they chose a different spot each time.

Once they climbed a hill and lay in a clump of trees, from which, when they stood up again, they could see down there the town, its main street with their offices in it and the evening sun on rooves. Richard said: "You know it would be all right staying here if you could be, like your Mr Hodges, a junior partner straight away. But it would take ages and we'd be quite poor meanwhile."

"We?"

"Well . . . don't you think . . .?"

"Search me," said Joan.

This evening at six, a mossy bank beside a stream and near a clump of brambles. Within three fields—a farm-house where dogs barked, cows mooed. Above them in the trees wood-pigeons cooed.

Joan had found in a sister's room at home a much thumbed book with diagrams. It was called *The Way to Sex Technique*. Advanced stuff, this, in detail. First chapter: Foreplay. Second chapter: The Erogenous Zones. Third Chapter: Contraception.

They used French letters which Richard sent for from an address they found in the *Daily Mail*. These came in plain wrappers every time supplies were low.

A mossy bank, but with some sticks and rabbit droppings first removed. And even then some bumps which could not be ignored until the furthest erogenous zones were reached. Beech leaves above them and some elm. Some stubby oak trees and a quantity of wild garlic which smelt most in May and during bluebell time. Dandelions of course and rabbit droppings because myxomatosis had not struck by then.

Richard buttoned up his trousers and his shirt and walked downstream, while Joan had her post-coital cigarette. She lay

10

on her back and watched the leaves move and thought of Mr Hodges.

Richard jumped across the stream and ran up the bank on the far side, then ran down again and swung hand over hand on an overhanging branch. He had been in the commandos in Malaya for his National Service.

"They say in the office," she said, as they walked back towards the stile, "that Mr Hodges got his wound on D Day plus one."

"What a tragedy for him," said Richard.

"Why a tragedy? It meant that he didn't have to fight again."

"For most people that would be a tragedy," said Richard.

"How can it be a tragedy to avoid bullets through your legs and arms or in your stomach or your balls? Smashed bits of bone and flesh. I would have been a pacifist or a conscientious objector."

"You're not most people," Richard said.

The best thing to be said about Mr Hodges was that he grew on you. He didn't seem anything at all special at first. He was pale and not particularly interesting. He seemed quite old, but that may have been his limp. And he was even slightly bald. But he was very nice to work for. Even quite bad mistakes on letters he was nice about. He would buzz his bell and send for you and apologise for asking you to type it out again. One of the other typists said he was good looking. "He's better looking than your Richard," she said to Joan.

"Well *I* don't think so," Joan said.

"Anyway, it's not important, is it? You might go away sometime." She imitated Joan's clipped way of talking.

"I jolly well hope I do, too," Joan said.

Strictly speaking, Richard *was* good looking. And her parents said so and her sisters said so. He had regular features and his hair was blond and curly. He was bony and athletic. The athletic side did not impress her but it had some value; he could lift her over difficult banks; he could even carry her through fields on his shoulders just for practice.

"Practice for what?" Joan asked.

"You don't think we are going to live through peace for all our lives?" he said.

11

"But if there was a war you'd be called up and you wouldn't be carrying me anywhere."

"I might be carrying somebody or something heavy."

" Anyway we'd all be dead with radiation next time straight away."

"A silly way to talk and unconstructive," Richard said.

Mr Hodges did not look as if he had ever carried anyone, apart from his two small daughters, of whom he kept a snapshot on his desk. They looked thin and unintelligent and you could not imagine them ever growing up and having careers.

The summer after Mr Hodges came to be a junior partner, Joan wore mostly dirndl skirts. She had at least half a dozen in plain colours, yellow, green, red, rusty brown and some of them she'd made herself. Her favourite was a lettuce-green, a most unusual colour for which she had bought the material in the market for 2/11d a yard. She also bought new sandals. These clothes were her office clothes; bare legs, new sandals, painted toe-nails and a wide elastic belt. It might not be as easy to feel well dressed in London or abroad.

Mr Hodges liked the green skirt and commented on it, which was the first time he had ever commented on her clothes. The other girls wore flowery dresses, but Joan felt better dressed because of the variations she could make with shirts and all her dirndl skirts. Her eldest sister, who had married an American, sent striped T-shirts.

"I like the green skirt," he stared as she came in to take dictation. "I like it very much."

"Oh thank you."

He gave dictation slowly. He was often at a loss for a word; an ordinary word like "condition" or "circumstance" often escaped him. He seemed distracted. Perhaps his tragedy on the Normandy beaches or the pain of it. He sat in shirt sleeves in the sun which came in through the grubby window and lit up the hairs on his wrists and arms. His arms were rather thin and weak. His skin never seemed to tan like Richard's.

"Dear Mrs Adderley . . . ," dictated Mr Hodges.

Joan waited. She sat opposite him across the office floor with a map of Dorset pinned to the wall above her head. The sun shone on to that.

"Yes, very nice," he said.

12

"What's very nice?"

He gazed at her; he wore glasses, pink-rimmed, National Health frames, and studied the paper in front of him. Something about the glasses made him frail. On days you heard him limping badly on the stairs, there were broken veins on his cheeks. If he would sun-bathe, be outside a bit more, these fragile cheeks would tan.

"Wake up!" he said.

"I am. I'm waiting."

"I was talking to myself." He slapped his own face. "Now, this letter to Mrs Adderley . . . dear Mrs Adderley . . ."

He had been on holiday this year—to his wife's mother's in Llandudno—and had returned looking just the same, still pale.

"Address it," he said, "to Mrs Adderley, Bottle Cottage, Hightown."

Joan sighed. "We'd got to the beginning of the letter . . ."

He took his glasses off and polished them on a handkerchief. Joan looked at her shorthand book; she had once seen his eyes without the glasses. They were grey, the grey of his demob suit, but there was some kind of transformation when he took his glasses off; it made you blink.

"Oh yes, I'm sorry. Dear Mrs Adderley . . . and head this . . . re extension at Bottle Cottage . . ."

"Re?"

"Yes, re . . . about . . . concerning . . ."

"You never write to Mrs Adderley about anything else; she'll know what it's about."

Mr Hodges sighed this time. "Exactly. Have it your own way then." He leaned back in his swivel chair.

"No, it doesn't matter. Honestly. Sorry."

He began again. "Dear Mrs Adderley; I am pleased to tell you, following our conversation yesterday that we shall shortly be forwarding the plans and estimates for your extension to the County Council Town and Country Planning . . ."

Joan made her shorthand outlines. Mr Hodges paused. Outside, the traffic went on through the town; not heavy; this was early-closing day and too early in the season for holiday-makers to be going west in numbers. Mr Hodges puffed on his pipe with a slight gurgling noise. Joan sat under the map of Dorset with her legs crossed, looking at her toe-nail varnish which was pillar-

13

box red today. She moved her feet, circling them in an exercise she'd read about in *Woman's Own* that would improve her ankle shape.

"Where was I?"

"Town and County Planning . . ."

"*Country* Planning."

"Sorry." She watched his feet from her side of his kneehole desk. He wore suede shoes with rubber soles, grey socks, grey suit and even a grey shirt today. It was difficult to tell with Mr Hodges if he wanted everything to match or if it was coincidence. Because none of it was very smart. Or perhaps, like some wives she had heard of and read about, Mrs Hodges put out every morning what she wanted him to wear. Joan's father's batman did that in the war. And Jeeves in P. G. Wodehouse.

"At next month's meeting of the Town and Country Planning Committee it is to be hoped that . . ."

"Hoped that . . .?"

Mrs Hodges was pale and blond and very small. And had been seen in distance only. She pushed a big, high pram with this baby in it and this older child sitting on the cover.

"Yours sincerely . . ."

"You usually put yours faithfully to Mrs Adderley."

"Yes, well, yours sincerely this time, please . . ."

You could not picture Mr and Mrs Hodges in bed together, although they must have been in such a situation well within the last two years judging from the baby's size.

"I've met Mrs Adderley several times now, you see . . ."

"I know. All right then. Yours sincerely."

"Thank you, Joan."

"You're welcome."

"Right then. Can we do another?"

"Yes of course."

Kath, the other typist, said he was good looking. Maybe once, when he had first met Mrs Hodges. But not now. He was very nice; that was all. Just nice, when he felt well, when his leg didn't hurt.

"To Messrs Ford and Moody, 23 High Street, Blandford . . ."

Kath said Mr Hodges was a lady's man. "I don't know what you mean," said Joan. "You *do*," said Kath. "Go *on*. It's in his eyes!"

14

But all that was in Mr Hodges' eyes was grey behind the glasses. And he smiled and was pleased to see you in the morning. "Dear Sirs . . ."
You never thought of him undressed or anything like that. You could not. Joan looked at her toe-nails, still circling her foot. She moved on the chair because her belt was tight; she eased it with a finger, then she put a hand inside her blouse and hitched her brassière shoulder-strap.
"We thank you for your letter of the 20th instant . . ."
In fact she thought of other people's pubic hair and sexual organs uncomfortably often. You could not go through life believing that, apart from Joan and Richard, everyone was like a rubber doll with Tri-ang stamped between their legs.
"And we confirm that it will be convenient . . . Joan?"
"Oh, sorry!"
"What's the matter?"
"Nothing, honestly."
"You're a funny girl . . ."
"We confirm that it will be convenient . . . ," Joan repeated slowly . . . "Why am I funny?"
"Never mind."
"I want to know."
"And we confirm that it will be convenient . . ."
He looked better when he was in the drawing-office next to this room. There, in shirt sleeves, on a high stool, he would bend, back to the high window over a sloping desk, with hinged ruler in his hand and pencil behind his ear. She yawned.
"Are you *so* bored?"
"No. Of course not."
"When I first came, you said you would be leaving soon."
"I suppose you want me to."
"No. Not at all."
"*You* think I ought to go away?"
"How can *I* possibly tell?"
"I suppose not really."
"Do you *want* to go?"
"I don't know."
"What about . . . er . . . what about young Richard? What does he think?"
"He doesn't count."

15

"I see!" He took his glasses off again and polished them on the end of his tie. He shuffled the letters to be answered into a pile and held them out to her across the desk. She got up from her chair to take them.

"What do your parents think about it? What do they think you should do?"

"They don't know. They have no idea what people ought to do."

She was wrong; her parents did know what people ought to do. They were competent successful people in their sphere of influence. They were both on councils and committees and her father had commanded troops in Normandy; not that part of the beach-head where Mr Hodges had received his wound, but had arrived there later, once the beach-head was established and had led tanks through Amiens and eventually into Paris. Now he was retired, successfully and happily, pensioned, and gardened energetically, built sheds and renovated walls and smoked out wasp nests. And her mother, equally, had moral principles and was full of energy and could give good advice if asked. It was simply that they both thought their children knew what they ought to do themselves. Three had married and the fourth was bound to do so soon.

Joan, when she came home that night, leaned her bicycle against the stone wall by the garage and wandered round the side of the long, low house, through the garden, down the path between the borders and stood beside the goldfish pond.

The Colonel, waiting for his dinner, looked out from the mullioned windows of the Old Rectory and said: "What the hell's that girl doing out there in the garden?"

"Oh darling," said his wife, "she's only mucking about. They all do that."

"She ought to get up off her bottom and make something of her life."

"But she *is*, darling. She is *working*. She has a *job*. I think the young are *very* enterprising these days."

Joan walked away down the long gravel path towards the kitchen garden and picked a few strawberries. Then she sat on the wooden gate and ate them. Then she came back up the path and past the pond. This way you could walk towards the

16

stone house and see the evening sun shine back at you from the upstairs windows; a great big ball of evening sun behind you and in front of you. She walked between her mother's climbing roses on the pergola, pink roses that came out white in bud and then, as they came into full bloom, were tinged with pink. She reached up and picked one just in bud and one in full flower. She had to pull the stalk quite hard, which pricked her fingers. She gave up pulling but the rose hung down; its stalk was broken. Her mother hated roses to be left like that. Joan gave another tug and made her fingers bleed. "Oh well," she said to herself, "what the hell?" Another tug. The climbing rose tore further down and came away. With a spray of roses in her hand she walked on out beneath the rustic arch which sagged under the weight of all that growth, and came on to the lawn. "I've picked you some roses, Mummy," she would say. And her mother would say, "Oh thank you, darling."

Her father watched her coming; then turned his back and went into his study to pour himself a whisky before dinner. Her mother dished up in the kitchen.

This evening Joan and Richard got off their bikes at the bottom of the steep hill where the road went in between high earthy banks with hedge-top elder trees meeting over it. In this tunnel Richard took both bikes and pushed them up the hill, leaning between with a hand in the centre of each pair of handle-bars. Joan followed him, some way behind. Her feet were dusty in her sandals and her red toe-nail varnish hardly showed.

Richard leaned forwards with his spine showing underneath his shirt and sweat between his shoulder blades. His hair gleamed in the tunnel when he crossed a sunlit patch.

She shouted from behind: "What are you practising for now?"

He answered without stopping: "I wasn't practising for anything in particular."

"Just showing off then?"

He went faster and ignored her.

"Just showing off that you can have sexual intercourse and still push two bikes up a slope?"

He stopped and waited for her; he was now practising how to be both angry and dignified. She reached him and walked

17

past him, between him and the yellow earthy bank which crumbled in dry heat and trickled down in places on the road. Having passed him, she felt his arm come out and grip her, holding on to her with that arm, leaning the two bikes against his body and securing them with his other hand. He pulled her towards her bike so that her green skirt swung against the oily chain. "Sometimes," he said, and paused. "Sometimes you can be rather unpleasant."

"Yes, I know."

"Very unpleasant, in fact."

"Yes I know. It's interesting. A lot of people are unpleasant. It causes wars."

She felt his hand twitch. He was about to let go of her arm and hit her. But he did not. He simply let her go and handed her her bike. He mounted his and standing on the pedals rode it slowly up the slope, bending forwards so that she could not see his head, but only his bottom moving well above the saddle, going on up towards the light which fell on the road where the tunnel ended. She pushed on slowly after him.

About one mile after the tunnel ended, the road forked. A signpost here said "GREAT GRIMSTONE 1" and "LITTLE GRIMSTONE 2". Great Grimstone was indicated to the left and Little Grimstone to the right. The banks were still high here, but there was a gateway just before the fork where you could rest your bike and wait. This would be where Richard would be waiting for her when his anger had subsided.

But he was not there. His bike was not leaning on the five-bar gate.

Joan put her head in the air and cycled on, forked left towards Great Grimstone along the flat road which went between white railings and wide grass verges. Down to her right beyond a field were willows and a stream, and beyond that again the road to Little Grimstone where Richard would be riding. Unless, of course, he had come this way and was lying in wait for her somewhere, to apologise.

Great Grimstone was in sight; the church tower jutting out between the copper beeches, and its flagstaff, white and empty, and the first cottages of the village street which stretched along in this direction. No sign of Richard waiting anywhere. She got off her bike and climbed the painted fence and looked across the

18

valley to the Little Grimstone road, over the willows and across three fields. He would be there somewhere. You could usually spot his head or the glint of his lowered chromium handle-bars. Her bicycle lay on the grass verge, wheels slightly moving. She went and sat beside it, and from her shoulder-bag she took her dark glasses and put them on. And found a Gold Flake cigarette and smoked it. The bicycle wheels ticked in the silence; wood-pigeons cooed as they did all day round here, and, from the village, smoke rose from the occasional stone chimney. The sun was turning pink and the sky was heavy with nothing in particular. Joan began to cry. Which was why she had put on her dark glasses.

The road was pale in front of her, and in the distance came a figure on a bicycle. But on a tall bike with straight handle-bars and with a bag hanging from them. A man in a cap was cycling towards her with his lunch bag on the handle-bars, not hurrying, because he always rode this way at that time of night and had done so ever since she could remember. He said good evening as you would to anyone along that lane. Joan nodded at him in her sun-glasses. She rubbed her face with her hand where tears had trickled underneath the lenses down her cheeks.

Smoking sometimes stopped you crying. So she found another Gold Flake and stayed beside the bicycle on the grass verge until she'd finished it. Smoking was one of the better things about being apparently grown up. That and sex, she thought. At least smoking stopped you sobbing.

When she came through the garden she came slowly to let her eyes dry out.

They ate in the stone-flagged kitchen at the back at eight o'clock. They ate on an old scrubbed kitchen table, but they used family silver and Crown Derby china. They ate with the window open because of the heat from the Aga cooker upon which Mrs Falconer had made soup and scrambled eggs.

At eight forty-five the Colonel consulted his half-hunter watch which hung on a chain across his waistcoat and said he had to go. There was a meeting at the village hall.

"Well, what would you like to do now, darling?" said Mrs Falconer to Joan.

Outside the window, clematis and honeysuckle clung and

19

climbed together over trellis-work which had been put there so that servants in the days before the war could not watch gentry in the garden.

"I'll wash up if you like," said Joan.

In the kitchen you were near the hall and near the telephone.

"How's Richard, darling?"

"I expect he'll ring."

The Colonel walked along the village street between thatched cottages with gardens stuffed with hollyhocks and stocks. He swung a walking stick, walked firmly, purposefully. He wore plus-fours and woollen stockings to the knee, and his summer linen jacket he had had for twenty years. His bald head glowed with sun-tan; he looked younger in the summer and could have passed for fifty. When he was fifty he used to pass for thirty in the heat.

The village pub, the Red Lion was an ugly building. Brick red, it spoilt the village street most people said. The Colonel slowed down here; not to go inside, but to say good evening to the six or so men leaning on the wall or sitting on the steps. He knew them all by name and what to say to them. At least he thought he did. They might laugh at him after he had walked on past, but that was no concern of his. People who worry about things like that do not get anywhere in life. He called them by their surnames, Turner, Spencer, Davies, Johns; they nodded, touched their caps and called him Colonel, their west-country accents giving the word a central "r".

Richard rang and Joan was feeling better. She leaned out of her bedroom window in the dusk and smelled tobacco plant. The honeysuckle and the clematis here reached her bedroom window and had to be pushed out of the way if you really wanted to lean out. Below her was the lawn, and in its middle the big copper beech with deck chairs under it. She could be feeling really happy at this moment. She supposed she ought to be. But she had no idea.

Mrs Falconer was listening to the wireless, an interesting play about some people in the war in Belgium, about the time of liberation. An English soldier was in love with a Belgian housewife, but of course it had to end, and it ended suitably and yet romantically.

Mrs Falconer was a big striding woman who never sat down for long. She got up from her chintz sofa and drew the curtains of the drawing-room and went to her bureau to write a letter to her oldest daughter in New England.

Joan thought: "It might be a good time to go away now." And decided to think about it in the morning.

Her room was dark and carpeted in faded green and had on its walls bright paper, illustrated. Winnie the Pooh and Piglet were everywhere; and on the curtains too. If Joan did not go away, she would make her parents change it.

Beside her on the window-seat were stuffed toy animals. These she would put away as well. Her mother said she must find mothballs and a wooden chest.

She gazed at Christopher Robin and Pooh dancing in the Enchanted Place at the end of the House at Pooh Corner. And then she picked up a book.

Sebastian Flyte in *Brideshead Revisited* had a teddy bear called Aloysius. And Sebastian Flyte drank himself to death and died quite young. Joan reached for the largest bear on the window-seat and lit a cigarette.

TWO

MR HODGES DID not live up one of the extremely pretty valleys near the town. He lived on the main road west out of it in a house in a row set back behind iron railings and a laurel hedge; the house was square and stuccoed white. Compared to the mullioned-windowed rambling houses in the villages, it might be called a boring house. But he liked it. It was the first house he had ever owned, and when he sold it, it would be because he had designed and built his own new house. This one he lived in now was clean and white and square with four windows at the front.

At the back there was a walled garden, the wall being old and weathered brick, a small lawn where his two small children played and a vegetable patch behind a flower border.

From the upstairs front windows you looked across the main road to a field which was a water meadow. From the downstairs windows you only saw the laurel hedge. This view depressed his wife, Winifred, frequently. Mr Hodges, who was called Ben, said it gave variety; closed in and cosy from downstairs and open spaces from upstairs. "I never have time to go upstairs," said Win, "and if I do, I have to carry the baby with me. Perhaps I've got claustrophobia."

Ben thought she was just homesick, miserable and bored with washing nappies; it was a passing phase; they would have no more children; that was more or less agreed. The two they had she worried about, considered, pampered; Win read Dr Spock in first edition. The second baby, breast-fed on demand, had been demanding ever since.

The drawing-room or lounge or sitting-room or front-room of the Hodges' house was bare. A large room with a pale wood floor and very little furniture, but with a mantelpiece of classical proportions, white carved wood with fluted pillars and a black iron grate.

On the other side of the front hall was his drawing-office, an equally big bare room with white walls; a square black table occupied the centre of the room, covered with plans and drawings. Ben came in through the front door and went out through the back door. He had walked home that day because Win had the car.

Ben walking, limping slightly, with his brief-case down the main street, past shop fronts, pubs and garages which in those days stretched their fuel hoses across the pavement. Ben, looking at the sky and whistling from time to time, his raincoat over his arm and going home to Win, examining as he went the rooves of dwelling houses, tiles or slates, considering the texture of old brick, stone surrounds of windows, new brick lintels, door designs, and changing daily his thoughts on building materials he would ideally use.

Ben, unprepossessing at this distance, slightly stooped and looking not always at the shapes of windows, doors and architraves, but also watching human shapes and sizes, people walking, standing, girls in calf-length dresses, belted tightly, swinging skirts or clinging pencil-slim skirts, high heels, low heels, thin ankles, fat arms, but mostly watching busts which were contained and firm. There were exceptions, but these were, sadly, older women drooping, who had never worn brassières. A variable mild wind might lift a skirt and show a knee, but nothing stirred the boning of the brassières. A breeze might just reveal suspenders.

She was in the garden with the children; sun and Win and children on the grass. In her sun-dress, small and freckled, thin with narrow arms and wrists with pointed elbows. Joan again was wrong; Ben could lift Win up and carry her along.

At the cinema they still held hands, and when they could afford a restaurant he took her out to dinner; she liked wine and would grin across the table. On the way home he would say "I love you, Win", and she would say, "Oh good. I still love you, you know. You are a very attractive man . . . know that?"

"It's nice to think that you still think so."

"I'll go on thinking so, whatever happens."

Win was a thoughtful person, given to deep reasoning of a complicated nature.

They were usually much happier when the children were not there. Except on rare occasions like today, just now, this minute. The late June evening, heavy like it was up in the Grimstone valley, was laced with diesel fumes from lorries driving west, but also laced with just a touch of sea air, salty from a mist which hovered south of Ben's house over the water meadow.

"And was it lovely on the beach?" he said.

"Oh, it was lovely, Daddy."

"Yes, it was lovely, darling."

"Oh good. I'm glad it was so lovely."

They'd been to the beach but were in the garden now, in the sunny patch beyond the shade of the lime tree; the baby in its playpen, quietly and unusually happy. The three year old, Fiona, was sitting on the swing and singing. She jumped to the grass, ran towards her father to be lifted in her bright pink shorts. Win came up to him, kissed him on one cheek while Fiona kissed the other. Family bliss, albeit temporary, could go no further, could it?

Weathered brick around them, vegetables succulent in neat rows, the lime tree at its best, and other trees from other gardens either side grown up above the walls and made the Hodges' moment not just warm and sandy but also leafy with birds singing.

The kitchen was in the built-on section of the house, built on and jutting out; so from it, as you cooked, you looked out on to the back garden. In winter it was colder than the rest of the house unless you kept the oven on and all the burners. In the summer, though, you had the window open as you cooked or scraped or peeled new potatoes at the sink.

They ate their meal in what they called the back-room; it opened from the kitchen and was where the children played and kept their toys. They ate at a table pushed against the window and they listened to the wireless, not to the play which Mrs Falconer heard, but an earlier programme than that, a concert on the Third Programme, while eating new potatoes, lamb chops and peas and looking out on to the lawn, the vegetables and the lime tree from the tall sash window, hearing music.

"It's Brahms," said Ben.

"It's nice," said Win.

"Or it might be Mendelssohn," said Ben.

He looked at her; she was enticing, freckled, curly-haired, as young and all the rest of it as the day he married her, as fresh as the day he first met her in 1947, neat wrists wearing the gold watch he gave her, familiar the way she held her knife and fork; delicacy but determination. He wondered what she'd look like when she was sixty, and, suddenly, with a piece of lean lamb from the chop on his fork, it struck him as it had never struck him, that they would still be together then.

"It doesn't matter what the music is," said Win.

He got up to fetch the *Radio Times* to check the symphony. To be with Win at sixty might be cosy, but the years between stretched out like this, like eating lamb chops, listening to the wireless, like not finding the *Radio Times* and saying: "Where's it gone? I suppose they've torn it up."

"Who's they?" Win had her elbows on the table, pointed elbows on the table-cloth, which, when she moved them, left an imprint on the cloth.

"The children, who else? Or hasn't it come this week? Or haven't we paid the bill?"

"It hasn't come, the paper bill. It hasn't come for months. It only comes occasionally—that's why it's so huge."

"Ridiculous!" He picked up a pile of papers. "We have too many papers." He pushed them along the floor; they spread about the carpet. He picked up a cardboard box of toys and banged it on the floor. He opened the toy cupboard, put the toys in, banged the door. "They should send bills. It's crazy. We pay and they don't even send the papers that we want."

"You often laugh at that, Ben. You often think it's funny. I've heard you admire their inefficiency. You think it's quaint. But why go on about the bill? Why not listen to the music? In the end you'll guess it or you'll hear the announcer say what it was." She reached to the mains set on the window-sill and turned the volume knob. Full orchestra burst out; the room was full of it; it might be Brahms; it might be anything. Ben dropped the pile of papers he was holding and crossed the room; to lean over the table and turn the wireless off.

"Oh come on, Ben. Don't spoil it. Please don't spoil it." Win sat where she had sat throughout in front of her empty plate.

25

She put her glass of water down, her fingers curled round the glass and only slowly did she move them and slowly turn her head to look out of the window where the sun had left the lawn and shone upon the wall and made it very rich and red. Ben stood across the table from her; the corner of her eye was full of him. Her shoulder which was bare was nearest him.

Sitting still is what she did on these occasions; sat exactly where she was and went on sitting. Either he would go right out or he would go into the garden, but since Win was looking into the garden, he would not go there. So it followed he would go right out.

He went into the hall; she heard him in the drawing-office. Now he would be pacing round the table. She sat still.

The office door was opened and his footsteps went towards the front door. This opened and this shut but was not banged. He was not a man to walk far. He would not go on to the road and walk, but go round to the side and take the car. She waited for the engine sound. It was a pity that, knowing so well exactly what he was about to do, she could take no satisfaction from this knowledge. She heard the engine start.

If he shot out of the concealed entrance on to the main road, he would have to shoot across the prevailing traffic. So he would shoot out left and, if he had to wait for traffic, he would make acceleration noises as he went, a noisy exit into town through empty streets and, with the sun behind him, eastwards.

He would stand on a hill or by a hedge and light his pipe and chew a bit of grass and stamp a bit, walk up and down, sit on a five-barred gate and scratch his bald patch, then come home.

Win got up, cleared the table, put the remains of Ben's dinner in the oven, relit the gas and left it turned on very low, a pyrex plate over the top of the lamb chop, peas and new potatoes.

But one day, he might go off like that and not come back. He would come back for his clothes and leave a forwarding address. And she would have to ring her mother up and tell her. Win and the children would move near to her mother's in Llandudno and she would refuse to talk about her life with Ben, but get some maintenance, and, if she ever married again, she'd choose someone she did not love.

She went upstairs to look into the children's room. They were both asleep, the baby on its face with its bottom in the air; it had pushed itself into a corner of the cot, so hard that the wooden bars had made an imprint on its face. And standing there, Win had some complicated thoughts about the nature of her marriage.

She went downstairs and took some sewing out and leaned across the table to turn the wireless on and heard the play that Mrs Falconer heard.

Richard was spending the evening with his mother because his father was away. He helped her wash up after dinner and then he went upstairs to fetch some fossils he had collected at the weekend. He also rang up Joan.

His mother sat beside a table lamp in the sitting-room and knitted. Richard carried several fossil-bearing stones downstairs; he fetched a bowl of water from the kitchen sink and took it on to the paved terrace outside the dining-room and scraped the Charmouth mud from some potential ammonites.

He thought of going to see Joan, but felt his mother might not be pleased if he went out.

He left the fossil-bearing stones beside the bowl and wandered down the garden. Then he went inside again and was about to go upstairs and put on his running clothes. His mother from the sitting-room called out that perhaps he'd like to join her for a drink: "You're very restless, dear."

Downstairs he mixed her gin and tonic from the cocktail trolley and poured himself a tankard full of beer.

"It's nice to be just you and I sometimes," said Mrs Pridaux.

Richard sipped his beer and crossed his legs.

"How *is* Joan, dear?"

"Oh very well, thanks, Mum."

"And is she out with . . . Is she busy this evening?"

"No, just at home."

"I see."

Richard stretched his legs and sipped his beer; his large feet moved on the loose rug on the polished floor.

"Straighten the mat a little, will you dear?"

The Hodges' younger daughter usually woke at ten and screamed for an hour or two. Tonight she did not. So Ben and Win went off to bed and made love. "I want to make you happy," he said as he lay over her afterwards with his two hands cupping her head.

"You do. Don't worry."

She never made the first move, but never actually refused him. She never wanted it to start with but she usually enjoyed it in the end.

"Oh darling Win," said Ben, "it's marvellous and wonderful. Oh, making love to you is all I want."

"I hope it is," said Win.

"What did you say?"

"I said, I hoped it was," and she put her arms around him because although she had not wanted it to start with she had enjoyed it in the end.

"Of course it is." He let her head rest back on the pillow and moved to lie beside her, put his arms around her body. A thought struck Win, but left her soon. Relieved, she went to sleep.

Ben, in the bathroom later, where he went on nights he felt she might not want him, stayed there for a time and thought of other women, girls in the street whose skirts blew up, of Mrs Adderley of Bottle Cottage on whose extension he was working. The drainage was a problem. Joan Falconer but peripherally crossed his mind.

"She's very young," said Mrs Pridaux.

"Who, Mum?" Richard put his tankard of beer down on a small polished table.

"Joan, dear."

The beer from the tankard slopped.

"Fetch a little cloth, dear, from the kitchen, will you? As I was saying . . ."

"Joan's very adult, Mum. She knows her own mind."

"Yes dear, I'm sure she does."

"And she did get eleven O levels."

Richard, when he had fetched the dish-cloth, wiped the patch of beer. "She *is* eighteen." He leaned on the arm of the sofa, "And she . . ."

"Just take your weight off that, dear," Mrs Pridaux said. "Girls are less predictable than men." She took the cloth from

28

him. "What were you going to say, dear, about Joan?"

"Oh nothing much."

"Good looks and intelligence are not everything of course."

Ben in his blue pyjamas sat on a high stool in his drawing-office smoking his pipe, in front of him the plans of Mrs Adderley's extension; floor plan, elevation, drainage. Drainage was the thing to work on at this time. Pipes from the new Adderley bathroom here, pipes from the Adderley toilet, stand pipe here, pipes joining there. Existing position of the septic tank.

Bottle Cottage was in a valley; there was water from a well, electricity with which to pump this water up to the tanks. Mr Adderley was disabled in a wheel chair and the extension was for his ease, and hers. A downstairs bedroom and a bathroom, a wide opening in the original outside wall through which the wheel chair could go smoothly, a big wide window called a picture window looking out on to the Adderley lawn, the Adderley orchard, and beyond all that the stream which was the boundary of Bottle Cottage fruit farm.

Last year, reaching for an early Worcester apple at the end of August, Mr Adderley fell and was found by Mrs Adderley, supine, broken-spined. This year, as well as nursing Mr Adderley, wheeling him, helping to haul him out of bed on a winch mechanism, Mrs Adderley would have to pick the apples.

The front elevation of Bottle Cottage as it now existed; here the windows, here the door, the front door out of which she comes and stands, large breasted, flowing skirted, staring at Ben as if she cared with all her depth about his every word.

Ben smoked his pipe and concentrated on the drainage. Upstairs he heard the baby crying and Win's footsteps cross the passage.

"I'm going for my run, Mum."

"All right then, dear."

He had his running shorts, his singlets and his plimsolls, an old and greying pair, and he went out of the gate into the empty lane and ran along the top road which linked Great and Little Grimstone. Here were low hedges on the upward slope; his jogging head was visible from surrounding fields in the twilight as he jogged.

29

This was ideal running weather; the temperature being about 65 degrees Fahrenheit, some high cloud, but an occasional shaft of setting sun on tops of hills around him, highlighting a clump of trees here, a field of wheat there, still green but turned yellow as the shaft crossed and went on to a hedge top or a grazing field, and picked out a group of brown and white cows or a shaggy pony standing flicking flies with its tail.

Up the curve of the low-hedged road with the house behind him, he ran and ran along the top, and at this stage he knew that he could run for ever if he wanted to. And where there was no hedge, his own attenuated shadow fell and floated behind or beside him on the road.

This way he'd run at school in cross-country races and in the army when he'd run for his battalion. This way he had been fit enough for the Malayan Jungle and would be fit he hoped if called again.

This time it might be for a march to Moscow. In the winter he was even fitter. He never wore an overcoat; he had no gloves or scarves. He'd put an icy hand on Joan and she would scream. In the winter Richard had his own cold war to fight and win. "Mind over matter," he said to Joan one day.

"It's all very well," she said, "but when it comes to sexual intercourse, you're just as concerned with matter as is anyone."

He jogged. A narrow footpath to the right led off the lane and towards the top of Grimstone Hill which looked down on both villages. With long grass on either side, this was a steep and rutted track, pitted by tractor wheels. Here you must watch your feet on sharp ridges of dried mud, but still run in between the banks. He could have been a soldier all his life and gone on running for the battalion, but he liked it here; he liked the place his parents had retired to.

"And if you are practising for Russia," Joan once said, "you can't be as optimistic as you say you are about the future."

"You bear the possibility in mind," said Richard, "but you don't let it change your life."

The track was opening out; it ended; here was softer turf with rabbit droppings, tussocks and steeper than before. Now he was climbing, clutching bracken stalks to haul him to the top. He might have gone to read law at University, but he failed on Maths and English. His mother and his father said that being

30

articled was a more thorough training anyway. There was nothing, his father always said, like starting at the bottom.

The top of Grimstone Hill, when you reached it, was quite flat, 600 feet above sea level and like a platform looking down on tree tops near and other hills less near and other dumpy, dusky hills and misty hidden valleys. He might have stayed behind in Nottingham and taken a place in his father's business. But that was sold, a limited company now, and Richard's brother-in-law was there to protect the family interest. And Richard did not want that sort of life.

He saw pink in the western sky beyond Great Grimstone where the sun had set and to the east saw the main road where it ran high along flat hills and pinprick car headlights moving. He allowed himself five minutes here on top, sitting, as athletes sit after the race, head hanging down between raised knees, back heaving.

Another thing he might have done: he could have been a doctor, but his father said that the National Health Service had put paid to doctors' hopes these days. And if he had not come to live in Dorset, he would not have met Joan, and, difficult as Joan could be sometimes, she seemed to have a need of him. He did not want to live in Nottingham. He wanted real country; not a suburb. He wanted, if not wider scope and fighting, hills and sea and Joan.

Another thing he might have done was to emigrate to Australia.

Beyond the hills and valleys in the undefined space which was the Channel, Richard saw a ship light flicker.

And England, whatever his father said, was not, to Richard, finished. Earlier this month there had been the Coronation and the Ascent of Everest. And earlier this week the first Test match and we had nearly beaten the Australians. A cease-fire in Korea was now being negotiated and the Gloucester Regiment had taken the title Glorious.

Five minutes and he stood and started down again. His legs, though tanned, flashed white in growing darkness as he reached the road and took his jogging pace between the fields. The Rosenbergs, atomic spies, were executed yesterday. You had to see the world as safe.

Scion of the puritan ethic, Richard, whose father always said

31

that honesty was the best policy and good service to the public must prevail, that private enterprise could do no wrong and you put into life what you got out of it and got out what you put into it. But now with Nationalisation, capital itself was threatened and a sound profession might be good sound common sense.

"But Dad, you said that now the Conservatives had got back in . . ."

His mother answered that: "We live in a democracy, dear." But he still might think about Australia.

Mrs Pridaux, knitting behind the lattice windows of the nice mock-Tudor house on the edge of Little Grimstone, listened for the return of Richard, the heavy step and panting.

In his early days she read that bottle feeding should be stopped by eight months at the latest; she hid the bottle then and forced small bits of bread and butter, mashed potato also, into Richard's mouth. Thumb-sucking should be prevented at all costs; she bound his arms, and later, when he was on solids and never moved his thumb towards his mouth, she tied him to a chair and cut his golden curls. And later still, roaring and screaming, he was driven by her off to prep school where his energy was diverted into sport. Head down, prop forward, good solid scrum weight, Richard flourished.

This evening she picked his sweat-soaked singlet from the bathroom floor and put it in the linen basket with a sigh.

THREE

IN THE MORNING rain Ben drove to work, parking the car in the main street outside the office. Water dripped from the top of the tall stone building on to the pavement. He turned his raincoat collar up and went into the wide hall and up the echoing stairs. He paused on the first floor outside the typing office. The chatter in there was of Joan and Kath. The smell in the building was of carbon paper and wet clothes. The walls were grey, the sky through the window on the stairs was grey, and as he went into his office, he saw grey slated rooves across the street.

His leg ached, but not badly. He hung his raincoat on the hook on the back of the door and sat down in his swivel chair. The ache would ease; it might bother him more in old age, the doctors said. The original agony he remembered, and remembered screaming and deciding God was not around and never had been if such pain existed. He said to Joan once: "Do you believe in God?"

"I don't know."

"A lot of help you are."

"Do you?"

"God knows."

Joan laughed a lot at that. "I remember now," she said. "I am an agnostic or, I think, an atheist."

He switched the light on in his office. A pile of correspondence faced him, each letter attached to its appropriate file; he looked out of the window. Opposite, the Old Swan Hotel had lights on too, and maids were cleaning rooms.

Joan came in when he buzzed. Her hair was wet, combed back and into the nape of her neck where the permed ends curled up suddenly like cup hooks. The hair itself, usually dark brown, looked almost black. More lipstick on than usual, rather dark

B   33

red lipstick, black high-necked jersey and red cotton skirt which reached half way between her knees and feet. She came in from the dark corridor and stood just inside the door.

"Er . . . dictation please, Miss . . ."

"What?"

"I mean, Joan. Sorry. Letters please. Yes."

She looked around the room. The chair she sat on usually was out of place; it had been put by the cleaner underneath the window. She went to fetch it, tipping it; some rain ran down its wooden seat.

"Oh dear," said Ben, "shall I . . . look . . . I've got a handkerchief . . . we'll dry it . . ."

"It doesn't matter; I've been sitting on a wet bike saddle." She wiped the seat of the chair with the sleeve of her black jersey and sat down, crossed one knee over the other and pulled her black elastic belt so that the buckle was in front. The brightest thing in the room that morning was her toe-nail varnish, her lipstick and her skirt.

"It doesn't seem like summer any more," said Ben, "Does it really?"

"No, not particularly." She turned back the cover of her shorthand notebook.

"Right. This letter is to Hall and Hall of Bideford; you can get their address from the file."

"68, Fore Street," said Joan.

"Oh, right, yes . . . 68 Fore Street. Our reference . . ."

"PK 67835."

"Right. Yes. Dear Mr . . ."

"Pinkney . . ."

"Right. Dear Mr Pinkney. Thank you for your letter of the 15th instant, and I was glad to hear that, since our meeting, some progress has been made with this affair . . ."

"This what?"

"Affair . . . this business then."

"OK. All right then, business," and she changed the outline.

Ben yawned. He looked at the map of Dorset over Joan's wet head. Dorset, an approximate triangle with points at Bournemouth and Lyme Regis and a peak at somewhere in the Blandford district. He put his elbows on the pile of files and letters. The ceilings of these top floor rooms were low; rooms should not be like this. He reached for his engagement diary. This day was blank. He picked up a pencil and pencilled in the space which was for the afternoon. "Remeasure drainage, Adderley's," and hoped it would stop raining.

Joan waited, also yawning.

"Dear Mr Pinkney . . . ," and he paused again. Joan drew a range of mountains in the top margin of her notebook.

The telephone on his desk rang; he reached for it. "Hodges here. Oh hello, darling."

Joan went on drawing mountains, listening. Sometimes she gazed out of the window, sometimes she looked at her toe-nails. She had painted them this morning deep plum red. If she shifted her foot, the sandal would move slightly and reveal pale patches where the foot was not tanned. She had not very nice feet on the whole and perhaps she should not draw attention to them. She had been in here half an hour and had taken half a letter.

"Yes, darling, yes of course," Mr Hodges said into the telephone. "Yes I'm fine. I'm perfectly all right. Are *you* all right?"

Joan turned a page and drew another range of high-peaked mountains with her fountain pen.

He kept on saying: "Yes I'm fine."

She put a range of even higher sharp-peaked mountains behind the first range and decided that Mr Hodges was in pain this morning. And drew another range of distant mountains and decided that he had been in pain all night.

"No, it wasn't just the noise; I just felt restless."

A night of pain and sleeplessness it must have been. Most people would have missed work this morning, but he had to come; his money must be earned. Being short of money was bad enough for people like Joan who wanted to buy clothes all the time and have a motor bike one day, or for people like Richard who wanted a car as well. And for everyone who wanted to go abroad on holiday. Mr Hodges only had the old car, one white shirt, the grey and several blue ones, and the old khaki one which he wore today, frayed at the collar and cuffs.

She stopped drawing mountain ranges and watched him put the telephone down and yawn again. How awful to have awful clothes because you were buying clothes for other people, for your wife and children. In the time of clothes rationing, Joan's mother went without to buy the children more. That was

35

pathetic; seeing her wear the same old coats and frocks and skirts and shoes for years.

He picked up the letter and began the one to Hall and Hall again. He moved the swivel chair and put his legs up on the desk.

People faint with pain. At school Joan, suffering from toothache, fainted once; you went away and woke up sleepy on the classroom floor with a mistress loosening your school shirt at the collar.

Joan could loosen Mr Hodges' shirt when he fainted. Pity it was the khaki one. Perhaps he would tip his swivel chair and fall towards the filing cabinet. If Mr Hodges died, that would be sad, and she would go away.

In the typists' room Kath was using the Gestetner, turning the handle fast; letters to all clients sent by the senior partner, Mr Puller. Kath's way of using stencils made them clear and strong. Because she worked for Mr Puller, her typewriter was the best, a German one. Kath often said her dad would not approve of this.

"Why not?" said Joan.

"Well . . . you know . . . remember . . . do you?"

"Oh the war, you mean. No one thinks like that about the Germans now."

"You ask Hodgekin what he thinks with that piece out of his bum."

"It's not . . . it's not there . . . it's in . . . it's in his thigh . . . I think."

"Seen it, have you? Oooooo!"

"Of course I haven't seen it."

"Bet he'd like to show it to you . . . my grandad was always showing people his wound from the trenches."

"I don't suppose that that was in an embarrassing place, though."

"An emberressing place! Emberressing? Emberressing? Do you go on like that with Richard? Bet you've seen all his emberressing places."

"That's different," Joan said. She sat down to type out all that Mr Hodges had dictated. And that wasn't much. At least twelve letters left he hadn't answered. He might be up there now in pain, or having fainted.

Kath, still at the Gestetner, went on saying how her dad and grandad hated every German in the world, so she'd be off her head to tell them that she used a German typewriter.

Joan said that one of her sisters went out with a German prisoner once, after the war however."

"What a tarty lot you are then," Kath said.

"I was only trying to make a point about the Germans."

"Bet they made a point with your sister."

"Most nationalities did," said Joan.

The sun came out for a little while that afternoon when Ben drove up through Great Grimstone, past the Old Rectory and the church and took the lane north-west on up to Hightown.

No town at Hightown, only a pub, a farm, some cottages and a chapel. Beyond that the lane curled higher, as high as Grimstone Hill where Richard ran at night, and off this road there was a rough track down to Mrs Adderley's.

Bottle Cottage was a tiny place, two rooms upstairs and two downstairs. It had a lawn in front, and orchard to one side and that was that. Ben drove slowly in his 1930's Hillman down the rutted lane and stopped on the concrete space beside the cottage. He got out of the car and sniffed wet grass, clean mud and hay from several fields away. He reached into the car and fetched his brief-case out and his folio of Bottle Cottage drawings.

She stood outside the door on the little concrete path between the house and lawn. Her arms were folded; she often stood like that, strong arms supporting bosom. "Hullo," she said, "and welcome."

Mr Adderley in his wheel chair was way down there on the lawn; you could see the top of his head. "He's asleep," said Mrs Adderley.

She wore strange clothes, flowing flowery skirts and floppy blouses. Her long thick hair was tied back with a chiffon scarf. She always gave Ben coffee from an enamel pot on the kitchen range, and she sat at the wooden table facing him with the plans for the extension in between them.

"Just a few problems with the drainage," Ben said.

She leaned across the table and her breasts inside the white material, contained by something else beneath which could not be a brassière, swung above the plastic table-cloth. Her bulk

37

between Ben and the window cast a shadow over the plan.

"Just the position of the septic tank," said Ben, his eyes on where her nipples showed in detail through the material. Her arms supported her, thick wrists and forearms, fleshy upper arms, she towered above the table and the drainage plan and said perhaps he'd like to measure up again.

She followed him and stood nearby outside, arms folded, leaning against an apple tree trunk while Ben measured, bending, moving, making notes. "It was just a question," he said breathlessly, "of keeping the extension well clear of the septic tank and yet allowing sufficient space for pipes. To do with by-laws."

"Yes," said Mrs Adderley. "You look exhausted."

"It was touch and go whether we might have to move it."

"But we don't?"

"No, luckily."

"You do look tired," said Mrs Adderley.

The lines of apple trees with fruit just formed on them spread down the slope away from them. The grass between the lines was short and scythed by Mrs Adderley. At the far end the apples would be Worcester so she said, but here, the nearest end, Beauties of Bath which ripen earliest. An apple leaf is shiny on the upper side and dull beneath; a breeze will show first one side and then the other. They walked between the trees, both sometimes ducking heads, avoiding twigs and leaves and embryonic fruit and talked of how the blossom was this year, of dates of harvest, dates of building, planning permission from the County Council and of down-pipes, window-sills and plastic floor-tiles. But he always left Bottle Cottage feeling that a lot more had been said. He felt soothed and young. It was like visiting his parents, but without the guilt that brought of knowing that he had not done as well as they expected.

In the film of the recent Coronation, Ben saw Queen Salote, colossal Queen of Tonga, beside the little King of Ethiopia. With Mrs Adderley, Ben felt like that, like Haile Selassie and about to be devoured.

"What I think matters in a woman," said Mrs Pridaux to Joan that evening, "is common sense and friendliness, more than anything."

"Oh really?" said Joan.

38

"Yes I do. That's why we are so proud of Sally."

Joan sat uncomfortably on the Pridaux sofa, drinking sherry; it seemed to her that everyone was proud of their children. "Sally's very nice," she said.

"I'm glad you like her. She likes you, I'm sure. Sally's interested in people."

Joan put her sherry on the small round mat provided and tried to think of someone who was not interested in people, then remembered that her own mother was extremely interested in cats.

"Good looks, intelligence are all very well in their place but common sense and friendliness and . . ."

"Yes of course."

"And humour of course and dress sense. Sally buys such pretty summer dresses . . ."

Joan looked through the lattice windows at the blue sky and hoped that Richard would come home soon.

"She's not particularly interested in fashion . . ."

Joan looked at the clock; she'd been here twenty minutes.

The picture that she wanted of herself that year was this: the narrow waist, tight belted, narrow shoulders and prominent but perky breasts. The skirt should flare to calf length and the legs, where visible, be neat and end in little shoes with little heels; the ankle should be turned, in ballet fourth position almost; many people wore ballet-type low-heeled shoes, and trousers were tight and drain-pipe just as ballerinas wore as tights, and clung to ankles. And, if your skirt was pencil slim, it curved close over your bottom and clung to evidence your thighs.

It had not been easy getting ready to go to the Pridaux's this particular evening.

Her hair she wanted short and curly at the back, as anyone would who'd seen Mary Martin in *South Pacific* washing that man right out of it. The hair was difficult, so were the narrow shoulders, perky breasts and little feet.

An hour ago she stood by the mirror on her mother's wardrobe in the long dark bedroom where the three cats lay on her parents' bed, and she stood fourth position in her only cotton frock, which would, her mother said, be suitable for dinner at the Pridaux's. It was pink and flowered with round neckline and

39

its skirt stood out as wide skirts should and reached exactly where skirts should and fitted at the waist and had been much admired that summer at a cocktail party, at a garden party and at a fête.

She aimed to take it off, however, and reached a hand to the zip at the neck at the back and pulled. This stuck half way down between her shoulder-blades. She pulled; she called her mother who was in the garden picking the strawberries which Joan would take to the Pridaux's. She ran down there, down the garden, dress flapping from her back. Her mother said, "I can't see without my spectacles", but tried with juice-stained fingers and said "Drat" and "Bother", even "Damn", and how much better buttons, hooks and poppers used to be. "You'd better pull it up again and wear it."

"I was going to take it off. I wasn't going to wear it after all."

"Well, you'll have to now."

"I want to wear my new black trousers."

"Oh. Joan darling, honestly!"

The dress lay on the floor of Joan's room for a day or two until it was bundled in a cupboard and forgotten. The zip was jammed and torn away from the material. Joan went to the Pridaux's that night in narrow black trousers, black belt and white wrap-over shirt; a little red chiffon scarf tied round her throat. The effect she believed to be Byronic.

In the mirror again before she left she stood, arms folded, then arms on hips. She leaned forward slightly, letting cleavage slightly show. She sat on the floor cross-legged. This worked. She put her chin in hands. This also worked. Correct effect as long as you kept your face in the right position, kept it serious, thoughtful, enigmatic, cynical. Lie on the floor on your side, rest head on arm; equally successful. Legs stretched out, toes pointed.

Even if they did not approve, the Pridaux would be bowled over by this picture.

Her mother put the strawberries in a paper bag and Joan got on her bicycle.

The Pridaux's house was unlike any other house Joan knew. It was in the country, but was not like a country house. Between its bordering beech hedge, which shut it off from fields and lanes, there was no piece of ground uncared for.

"How nice of you to come," said Mrs Pridaux as if Joan was a stranger from abroad, and shook her hand.

Inside the Pridaux house everything was beige; that is to say that everything which was not polished wood or brass, was beige; beige velvet curtains, beige pelmets hiding curtain rails, beige carpet in the hall and on the stairs. The chairs and sofas were not beige, but very near it, having oatmeal-coloured covers.

"Richard's popped to meet his father at the station," Mrs Pridaux said. "Do you want to wash your hands, dear?"

Joan handed her the bag of strawberries, stained with red outside, and said she did not, thank you, want to wash her hands.

Mrs Pridaux wore beige as well that evening; beige linen with a white belt. She had white hair and sun-tanned skin because, like Mrs Falconer, she spent a lot of time in the garden. But Mrs Pridaux's hands were pale and smooth because she used her gardening gloves more regularly than Mrs Falconer, who scrabbled at the earth and roses and wore the fingers out of gloves and went on scrabbling and moving stones to make a rockery whenever it came into her mind to do so.

You moved quietly in the Pridaux's house and did not raise your voice. You sat down in the drawing-room and Mrs Pridaux poured you sherry. You sat feet folded under you because the outfit suited you that way, until you saw her staring at your feet and put them on the floor and crossed them at the ankles.

"It's nice to have a chance to chat," said Mrs Pridaux, "How is your mother?"

"Very well." Joan took a Gold Flake from the packet in her bag.

"You'll find a little ashtray just beside you. And your sisters?"

Beyond the lattice window was the beech hedge, pale spring green still, beyond that, blue sky. Joan looked out of the window and said her sisters were all very well.

"I expect you miss them, don't you?"

"Not particularly." Opposite the window, to Joan's left, a polished escritoire with glass-fronted bookcase on top; behind the glass were books with matching backs. And in the glass her own face mistily looked back at her. "No, not much," Joan said.

"I see. It was nice of you to bring the strawberries; you can help me wash them in a minute."

"We don't wash them; we just eat them," Joan said. In the bookcase glass her eyes looked dark, her hair was brushed back and had stayed that way in spite of the bicycle ride. In the Pridaux's house you sat quite still, except when you moved your arm to reach the ashtray or you lifted your sherry glass or put it back exactly on the mat.

"We're hoping Sally will be here for a visit later in the summer."

"Oh. That's nice."

"So you must come over then as well."

"Oh thanks. Oh thank you. Yes."

In the Pridaux house the pictures on the wall had matching gilt frames and were prints of Nottinghamshire and were spaced with equal spaces. There were brass fire-irons, brass guard, all polished. On the open escritoire were letters under paper-weights and headed writing paper. On the window-sills in front of lattice panes were ornaments of Staffordshire china, animals like cows and greyhounds. No cats to knock them down in this house.

"And how is everything at the office?" Mrs Pridaux said.

"Oh all right, thank you."

"I like the way you girls all work now. You enjoy it, don't you?"

"It's all right," said Joan, "but it can be very boring sometimes."

At Green Pastures, as the Pridaux house was called, the clock under the glass dome on the mantelpiece said seven forty-five and ticked as its pendulum swung. Mrs Pridaux poured herself another gin and tonic, slipped the lemon slice in with tweezers, looked at the clock and sat down again.

"Sally loves her work," she said.

The Pridaux Humber nosed its way through overgrown lanes from Yeovil Junction where Mr Pridaux had arrived from Nottingham. With Richard at the wheel, who heard how business was and could be if it was still run properly. Mr Pridaux had his doubts, but talked no more about the business. Instead he asked how his tomato plants were and whether Richard had watered them last night and left some greenhouse windows open.

In his grey business suit, Mr Pridaux loosened his tie and turned the window down, told Richard a joke he'd heard in the Conservative Club in Mansfield about Aneurin Bevan.

He hummed, as he often hummed, tunes from Gilbert and Sullivan, songs he had sung for the Mansfield Amateur Operatic Society, and said it was good to be home again. The only bad bit of his visit was the journey. British Railways meals were 12/6d now and rotten food. The carriage from Nottingham to St Pancras was filthy. Perhaps he would drive another time, would take the car. "And how is Mum?" he asked.

"Oh fine, I think."

"And cheerful? Is she bobbish?"

"Oh yes."

"Oh good. Well that's all right then." Mr Pridaux hummed again.

Joan sipped a second glass of sherry and heard how Sally loved her work, how Sally, married and with a house to keep, still went on teaching, loving children, loving teaching in a primary school.

Then Mrs Pridaux went into the kitchen, checked on the casserole in the oven and the vegetables and came back. She told Joan that Sally, even though not good looking, took care how she dressed, saved up for good clothes, washed her own hair and did not have a perm. Sally was never idle for a minute, Mrs Pridaux said. Even when she came home and was on holiday, she'd say: "Mum, may I make a cake?" or "Mum, shall I do the shopping for you?"

Mrs Pridaux's face changed when she talked of Sally, and Joan's grew longer along the lines she'd chosen by the mirror in her mother's room at home.

"I know!" said Mrs Pridaux, "I know what we can do," she said, getting up with great enthusiasm, as if the thought had struck her with such strength that it could not but enthuse Joan equally. "I know! Shall we have a go at washing those strawberries now?"

Dinner was in the dining-room which had french windows leading on to the terrace. The table, polished highly, reflected glasses, silver, faces. White table-napkins in silver rings; you drew them out and spread them on your lap. There were oval table-mats to

43

put hot plates on, round mats for glasses. Mr and Mrs Pridaux sat at either end and Joan and Richard faced each other.

"I do hope lamb casserole will be all right for you, dear," Mrs Pridaux said to Joan.

"Oh yes, of course."

You spread the white napkin on your knee and waited. You were served first, but you waited.

"Wine, young Joan?" said Mr Pridaux.

"Yes, thank you."

They ate the casserole and heard about the business and the journey.

"These strawberries have turned out quite well," said Mrs Pridaux. "Joan helped me wash them, dear." She leaned across the table towards Mr Pridaux.

At the Pridaux table you ate carefully and not too fast, lifted your table-napkin to wipe your mouth, sat up straight so as not to let the white shirt fall open.

"Good food at last!" said Mr Pridaux, and they all sighed over the iniquities of British Railways. Outside, the terrace, crazy paving swept, the oval lawn mown short with edges cut and round it pinks and carnations just in bud and leaning towards the centre.

"What do you think, young Joan?"

"Think about what?"

She felt Richard's foot press on hers under the table; he said, "about the nationalisation of the railways."

"But that was years ago," said Joan.

"An absolute disaster," Mrs Pridaux said.

Richard looked hopefully at Joan.

"The trains still go," said Joan.

"But do they go on time, dear?"

"Usually, it seems to me."

"Exactly, you have made my point," Mr Pridaux leaned towards her. "Usually!" He gave a sharp laugh, his eyes glinted in his sun-tanned face, his smile was as happy as when he sang the Major General's song from *The Pirates of Penzance*. "Nationalisation equals inefficiency."

"I'm sure it doesn't have to," Richard said, "I'm sure it could be made to work."

"I hardly think you know, dear," Mrs Pridaux said.

"Oh Mum! That's not fair . . . I *do* have *some* ideas . . ."

His father said: "You can't run a business with civil servants, Richard."

"Yes, but that's not the point," said Richard.

"It's a railway not a business," Joan said.

"Just cups of tea is all they want; if the profit motive's lacking, there's no more to say about it."

Richard's foot touched Joan's underneath the table again.

There was coffee on the terrace because the sun was out; they drank from tiny cups which rattled on the saucer as you held them. As the birdsong died and the sun went down in the direction of Great Grimstone, Mr Pridaux excused himself to water his tomatoes.

On the swing seat on the terrace, after Mrs Pridaux had also gone into the house, Richard had one foot on the ground and swang the seat gently; he held Joan's hand and then let go of it and held her knee. "I'm sorry."

"What about?"

"Well—you know," he nodded in the direction of the house and greenhouse. "They can't help it."

"Can't they?"

"It's just the way they are."

"They're just so sure they're right; it makes me spit."

"People can be like that when they're old."

"I don't see why."

They heard Mrs Pridaux's footsteps coming through the dining-room. Richard took his hand off Joan's knee and they sat staring straight out at the lawn. Mrs Pridaux came out and said, "and what are you two going to do now?" and went in again.

"They don't like me," said Joan.

"Of course they do. They know that you are beautiful and intelligent."

"And, even if I am, your mother spends her time saying that being like that doesn't matter anyway."

"Yes, but all the other things you are they like."

"And what are those?"

"Well, the things I love about you, I suppose."

"What are they?"

"Oh skip it, Joan. You don't ask things like that."

"I did."

He folded his arms, he looked at the sky; he stood with one foot on the parapet of the terrace. She swung the seat; one foot, one black-trousered leg she had tucked underneath her in the manner she had wished to sit all evening.

"I wouldn't mind," she said, "if they'd own up to having just opinions. But they make it fact!"

"You shouldn't ask me things like that," said Richard, "like what I love about you."

"You can let me know, if you like, when you have thought about it." The seat swung until it banged against the wall of the house. She said: "When I have a house I shall do exactly what I want in it."

Richard stood beside the seat and held it, stopped it swinging.

"I shall do exactly as I want and when I want," she went on, whispering.

"All right, all right, calm down."

"I shall eat what I want and when I want and out of anything I like, out of the saucepan on the floor if necessary. I might eat dinner in the drawing-room or in the bedroom. I might sleep in the kitchen if I felt like sleeping there. And anyone could come at any time and be allowed to do exactly what they liked at any time and say exactly what they thought."

"God help our children."

"Who said ours?"

The only thing she liked about the Pridaux garden were the magpies. Rather, she liked the gun they kept to shoot the magpies with. These twittered angrily and remained in the vicinity as a rule rather than in the garden itself. The .22 rifle Mr Pridaux bought for Richard years ago was put beside the french windows every morning.

The magpie threat was two-fold, first to the nesting box nailed on to the plum tree at the bottom of the garden, second to the plum tree fruit itself and to the fruit of other trees.

Joan had once been allowed to use it. She took it now and held the barrel to her shoulder. Richard hovered. "They'd rather you just frightened them and didn't kill them."

But the magpie, after the bang which resonated round the house and up the hill behind and was a commonplace sound to those who lived within gunshot hearing of Green Pastures, lay dead on the soft grass under the plum tree on a strip of grass this side of the beech hedge, its blue-black wings spread out, its white feathers glowing in the dusk and a dot of blood beside its eye.

FOUR

WIN AND BEN were in a traffic jam and it was hot. Through
the Hillman's sunshine roof the sun beat down on Win's head
and on Ben's bald patch. Fiona climbed on to the back of Win's
seat and stuck her head out of the roof and waved at people in
other cars; the baby moaned in its car-chair. They were on the
Exeter by-pass that Saturday midday on their way to stay the
night with friends.

Some people had stopped their cars completely and were
sitting on the grass verge waiting for the Saturday lunch-time
traffic to subside. If people left the home counties or left London
early in the morning on their way to Devon or to Cornwall, then
there usually was a traffic jam here at lunch time. The tarmac
sent back heat and petrol fumes were in the air.

Ben and Win, not having come this way before, had no idea
the traffic here would be so bad. Win said they should have tried
going straight through Exeter, but Ben said that was stupid; it
was Saturday and the streets of Exeter would be packed with
shoppers.

He sat in the driver's seat and turned his head towards the
left-hand verge. Two women had bikinis on and a teenage girl
was with them wearing linen shorts and sun-top. Ben watched
them covering each other with suntan oil, watched one woman
stroke it on the other's shoulders, watched another rub it on the
spine of the teenage girl and saw that the girl was looking back
at him.

Cars hooted; Win dug him with her elbow and he saw a space
in front of him; the cars ahead had moved a hundred yards.
Behind, cars revved up and a hot-faced man in a Morris 1000
directly behind the Hillman shouted, leaning out.

People in cars on holiday are crazy, Ben thought. Why did we

48

join them? Why come all this way? What is this life if full of care we have no time to sit and stare at girls in bikinis touching other girls?

Last night he dreamed a girl in a bikini had come into his office and had removed the top. He woke up, seized Win round the waist and held her to him. "Oh God," said Win, "not now."

The girl in his dream had dark wet hair. She was not Joan exactly, but someone he had once known well. He thought of all the women he had known, thought of them wet haired, coming out of baths, out of the sea, water running over necks and shoulders, trickling and dividing over breasts.

"People in cars on holiday are crazy," Ben said.

They stopped again; this time beside a girl in jeans who sat on the ground leaning against a car. She sat on a cushion with her legs apart and smoked a cigarette. Ben put the car in neutral gear and lit his pipe.

"Do look ahead," said Win.

"I am."

"You weren't just now. Oh honestly, Ben . . ."

"It's a harmless occupation."

"No it isn't. Honestly it isn't. People look back at you. They assume things."

"Good. I like assumptions."

"There's only one thing you like."

"What's wrong with that?"

"It's . . . it's . . . it's . . . excessive."

They drove at twenty miles an hour and Ben began to sing; he sang in French quite well; he sang "La Mer" and hoped he sounded like Charles Trenet, and he took Win's hot sticky hand and held it to his lips and said: "Cheer up. We're going to the seaside."

"Seaside," Fiona shouted from the back seat.

"Eeee . . . iiii . . . ," the baby copied her approximately.

In front of them a car was stationary; all cars were stationary. Ben stopped singing. There was no one on the grass verge here. He turned off the ignition and they sat. Win turned and wiped the baby's face with a wet face flannel from a sponge bag and gave it a drink of orange juice from its bottle.

"Oh bugger it," said Ben.

49

"I quite agree," said Win. She had dark glasses on and sweat on her forehead above them, and something running down her face which was either sweat or tears.

"Please darling," Ben said, "don't *you* get upset as well. It will be fun to see Geoff and Liz again."

Win wiped the baby's face again and her own face with a handkerchief. She leaned out of the window, looking forward at the row of cars and back behind at the queue and held the handkerchief to her nose because of petrol fumes and wished they had not come: "But still," she said, "we used to like them, didn't we?"

"Yes. Geoff's all right."

"Oh come on, Ben. You like Liz too."

The Morris behind them gave off steam from underneath the bonnet; the man got out and raised the bonnet.

"It's bad for the children, heat and fumes," said Win. "You liked Liz quite a lot in fact. You know you did."

"She's very . . . mmm . . . mmm . . . mmmm . . ."

"To say the least."

"Oh, she's probably gone off now."

But she had not gone off. She was slim and bony like a fashion model of the time and of most times within Win's memory. And Liz had been a model; she was dark and svelte and elegant when she bothered, which was not often since she mostly wore now shorts or slacks. In the heat she stood outside her seaside villa with a naked baby on her hip; her legs and ankles were as enviable as ever and her long neck as long and held as lightly. Geoff was beside her, blond and bronzed and bearded, wearing faded blue shorts and espadrilles.

The women kissed each other; the men shook hands and kissed each other's wives. They all admired each other's children.

There were sea-gulls high in the sky above this row of cliff-side houses with salt-cracked paint on windows, sand in drives and fuchsia hedges; tamarisk bushes and pines and palms edged the in-shore side of Clifftop Road.

The house was high-roomed, tiled floors, windows open, toys on floors and bathing towels on chairs.

"It's absolutely awful, ghastly," Liz said, "but it's known as home."

50

And through the house was a wide dry lawn and shrubs, a summer house and a grass bank hedging it from the cliff. The lawn was pitted and rough where Liz's sons had dug and burrowed in it. There were broken tricycles and push-carts and the smell of the sea, and, if you stood outside the smashed verandah of the villa you could see the sea, extremely calm today with yachts on the horizon.

"Where's the seaside?" said Fiona.

"Lift her up to see it, Ben," said Win.

"Let's have a drink," said Liz. "Geoff, get the wine." She turned to Ben and Win. "It's gorgeous to see you both. You look as good as ever, both of you. Let's lounge and drink. Let's let the kids get at each other."

Win held her daughters, one by the hand and one in her arms and stood there in the garden. You could see the sea and the land curving round towards Start Point and could hear the sounds of families on the beach below.

"Let's forget the kids and chat," said Liz. She threw herself on the grass and lay there stretching up a thin brown arm to take a tumbler of red wine from Geoff. She patted the grass beside her inviting everyone to sit.

"This is the life all right," said Ben, still standing up.

Win sat with the baby on her knee and Fiona standing at her shoulder.

"I've been looking forward to this like mad," said Liz, "Thank God we've got you here at last. The boys have been waiting for you all day." The small boys stood naked, staring at the group.

Fiona whispered into Win's ear: "When are we going to the seaside?"

Geoff squatted on the grass, holding the bottle of wine and filling glasses.

"Just like old times," said Liz.

It seemed to Win a funny way to spend an afternoon, just sitting, drinking, talking, instead of pushing prams and shopping, ironing, cooking.

Ben followed Geoff back to the verandah and the two men leaned there drinking.

"You haven't changed a bit," said Liz.

"I think I have," said Win. She got up to run and pick the baby from the top of the grass hedge where it had crawled.

"They never fall off," called Liz. "They get on top of it, but never fall."

Liz believed in letting her children do exactly what they wanted. There was no playpen in the house, no gate at the top of the stairs, no potty training, no bars at upstairs windows. The only locked place was the summer house where Geoff, a painter and a teacher of it, had his studio.

Liz lay on the grass beside Win and said: "Do you think you'll have more kids?"

Win said. "No, definitely not."

When Liz did not have the money for a chair she bought a cushion and put it on the floor. If a bed, she put a mattress down, and if a carpet, she would paint the floorboards. If Liz felt the need of indoor greenery and could not bother with a pot-plant, she would dig a shrub up from the garden and stick it in a barrel in the corner of a room. On the lawn her eldest son stood over her with a cup of water from the kitchen tap.

"I know they're bloody nuisances, but I think I may keep having them."

"Does Geoff agree?"

"God knows," said Liz, "but one must do something, mustn't one?" The son beside her poured the water on her stomach between the top and bottom halves of her bikini. "Sod you, Dominic," Liz said, not moving.

"I want to put on my bathing costume," said Fiona.

"Why don't you just strip off, love?" Liz said.

"I don't think she will," said Win.

The men walked past them down the lawn, wine glasses carried with them and went into the summer house. "That's Geoff's studio," said Liz.

"I usually," said Win, "let Ben cope with the children on a Saturday. It's his day with them."

"He *is* an angel," Liz said. "You are lucky."

"Geoff's all right, isn't he?"

"Not in that way," Liz said, "or in any way at the moment, come to that."

"Oh dear, I'm sorry," Win said, embarrassed, and she changed the subject. "Does he like the school?"

When Geoff and Liz and Ben and Win knew each other very well, they were neighbours in a block of flats, and, as young childless couples, they went out together in the evening, drank and danced and went to cinemas. Then they had talked of love and sex.

Liz stretched out in her bikini and said had not that been fun? The best years?

Win said yes, but saw that now, and rightly, properly, it was time to talk of children and of houses and of jobs.

Before the house was here, this summer house was here, a lookout post. Here someone came on what was called bad weather watch and here still were peep-holes for the telescope, hinged round portholes which could be latched from the inside; a view to the east and south and west of only sea. And on the floor, Geoff's pictures, pale nudes in greys and pinks and watery greens and blues.

They watched their wives pass down through the white gate to the cliff path, with children, towels and buckets and spades.

"Who are they?" Ben asked, looking at the pictures.

"Models."

"Are they . . . er . . . difficult to get?"

"Sometimes difficult to get rid of."

Ben gulped. "Really?" He faced south-west towards the point and saw a steamer moving diagonally north-east, a wash behind it, widening, heading between the yachts outside the bay. And on the floor, below this view, the flesh and breasts and sketchy pubic hair of girls Geoff painted.

"This one," said Geoff, picking up a picture of a girl reclining, mostly blue . . . "this one is Hazel. She's incredible."

"Yes, isn't she? And this one?"

"Ingrid. A large girl, Ingrid."

"Does she . . . I mean, one hesitates to ask, but do they . . .?"

"Sometimes . . . well . . . occasionally."

Ben held his wine glass, drained it, stared at the unframed flesh on canvas all around him, watched the steamer cross the sea and saw a plane come high up shining in the sun. And gulped again. "But . . . here, I mean? I mean . . . while you are painting them . . . or where?"

Geoff tapped the side of his nose. "Well . . . to be precise . . . about where you are standing now . . ."

Ben side-stepped and examined the spot on the dusty floorboards where he had been standing. "But I mean in daylight?

53

You can only paint in daylight. Liz could see . . . or doesn't she mind?"

"Twilight comes. And twilight at certain times of year arrives at children's bedtimes."

Ben saw that a female figure's breasts when she reclines, fall sideways slightly and that the shadow is beneath them. This was the figure, Hazel, thighs pale blue where the light was on them and a deeper Prussian blue in shadow. "Christ," he said.

"In fact," said Geoff, "I was meaning to explain, but Saturday is my day in the studio, the only time, apart from Sundays in the term. But Liz gets tetchy if I'm shut in here all Sunday . . ."

"You mean you'll be working here this afternoon . . . not Hazel or Ingrid?"

"No this one's Bridget; she'll be here at five."

"Does she . . .?"

"Does she what? Oh I see what you mean. I'm not that depraved."

"I just thought . . . ," said Ben, bending to examine where Hazel's stomach below the navel was purple darkening to black, "that perhaps I could keep the women amused indoors or keep them at the beach or . . ."

"Of course not. I'm just boasting really." And they went out of the studio and followed the women to the beach.

There were as many blues in the sea that day as there were on Hazel's or Ingrid's breasts and thighs. There were depths and shallows, rippled, rocks just under the surface adding green, shallows turquoise, distances of sapphire; all the colours Geoff could squeeze and mix from tubes of paint.

They walked on short dry grass and sea-gulls rose above them. The descent was winding, sloping, then in steps, and as you went lower you could see the reddish sand and children splashing in rock-pools and putting their toes in the smallest of all possible waves.

"Liz looks well," said Ben.

"She's all right now you've come. But she's been miserable, hysterical sometimes; we shouldn't keep having kids maybe."

"It's tricky when they're small."

"Mmmm." They walked one behind the other on uneven steps. Geoff, practised, going easily in his espadrilles, Ben picking his way behind him in old leather sandals.

"You do what you can," said Geoff. "It's rotten for them . . .
I don't know . . . I don't know, Ben."

"Perhaps in Liz's case she minds about . . . Ingrid, Hazel and
so on. . . ."

"Don't think it's that."

There was a flat stone, well above the beach, a flat white stone
which was heated by the sun and was there among the thyme
and heather, horizontally above the sea where you could sit and
see them at a distance, see the top of Win's head and of Liz's on
the sand, and not see which particular children were yours or
Geoff's, but see a lot of children moving, digging in damp sand
at low tide; paddling, buckets, beach umbrellas.

"Win looks happy anyway," said Geoff.

"I hope she is."

"Liz thinks you're perfect as a husband; she's always quoting
you and Win as perfect."

Ben sat there in the boiling sun, the white stone burning
through his trousers. "Loving," he said slowly "is, as someone
said I think, not quite enough." He unbuttoned his shirt and
peeled it off his back and felt the shock of the ultra-violet seaside ray hit on his spine and ribs. He looked down ashamed at
the whiteness of his chest, the softness of it and the extra flesh
around his waist, so that however much he sun-bathed there
would always be some unaffected creases.

"Tell you what, though," said Geoff, standing up, brown, lean
and everything that Hazel, Ingrid or Bridget would desire. . . .
"Tell you what, though, there's this woman, Laura, modelled
for me once . . . she has this amazing skin texture and. . . ."

Ben hung his shirt round his neck. He then bent down and
rolled his trousers up to just below his knees. He took off his
socks and put them in his pockets, carried his shoes and went
the rest of the way barefoot.

Little Dominic who was three-and-a-half stood naked in his
mother's kitchen. He was brown all over and had very dirty feet
and hands and face. He did not want to sit up at the table for his
tea like his little brother who was one year old and like his
friends who had come to stay.

The kitchen table took up most of the room but was large
enough for everyone except Geoff who was in the studio. Only

when Liz needed to reach the cupboard where she kept glasses, mugs and cups and saucers, did Ben have to move. He was placed next to his younger daughter, Amanda, who was also one year old; he was feeding her crushed banana and bits of bread and butter. It was his turn to do this on Saturdays and the visit made no difference to Win's schedule. It was the only time in the week he really looked closely at Amanda.

Amanda in the dictionary of names means: "Meet to be loved." Win loved her, Fiona seemed to love her sometimes and all four grandparents doted on her. Ben's feelings were more complex.

Liz in the kitchen by the cooker hitched the strap of her bikini top on to her sandy shoulder. She hitched the pants of the bikini up too, so that the curve of the buttocks which had been showing at the top was hidden, but the profile of the lower cheeks revealed.

Most of the crushed banana went on Amanda's chin and on her naked chest. You could not look at Amanda's torso naked without imagining, beneath the covering of pearly flesh, the frail structure of ribs and shoulder-bones and spine . . . and picture it crushed, unlike banana crushed. This was how Ben saw Amanda. Some emotion was aroused which was protective and intensely so. If a house caught fire and Amanda was in her cot on the topmost floor, however high the house, Ben would run through flames and smoke, holding his breath and bounding up quickly charring, crumbling stairs to reach her.

"I want some orange juice," said Dominic from the kitchen door. And Liz turned and reached up to a shelf to get the orange bottle, which action caused her bikini pants to slip again below her hip-bones.

If necessary, to save Amanda, Ben would jump and guide his body through the air with people shouting down below and holding blankets. He would jump and turn his legs up, clutching the thin weedy body which was Amanda's, free-falling he would aim his back, his spine towards the ground. Anything so that her birdlike bones would be held and shielded.

"I want some orange juice," Dominic said more loudly. Liz held her pants with one hand and reached the orange bottle with the other. "Sod you Dominic," said Liz.

And Ben, if still alive, would spend his life in a hospital's
56

spinal unit with a plastic bag permanently on his penis; no urge could be in that spot any more. And he would listen to the wireless, Brahms and Mendelssohn till kingdom come with no erection ever. All for Amanda. Whose fists waved at the end of twiggy arms and pushed handfuls of banana from the spoon, while Win across the table firmly looked away and knew that she must let him get on with it and not mind what a mess was made of it on Saturdays. And let Liz see that she was not downtrodden by her children and her husband and made them do things for her sometimes.

"Excuse me, Ben," said Liz and stretched above him towards the cupboard, reaching for a mug for Dominic, between Ben and Amanda. Amanda's banana-covered fist punched forwards, hit Liz on the right breast, spread gooey pale stuff on the brown skin. This stuff dripped down from brown to white untanned skin within the shadow of the bikini top. This, Liz pulled back and put in her hand and with one finger scooped the teaspoonful of crushed banana from her nipple. Ben stared.

"Pass that dish-cloth, love," said Liz to Win. She wiped her small dark nipple with the cloth and threw the cloth towards the sink. "And sod you once again, Dominic." She looked around. "Where is he, then?"

"He's gone, I think," said Win. "He's gone into the garden, I suppose. Shall I take the drink and find him?"

"No," said Liz, "no, definitely not. I'll go."

They heard her calling Dominic outside, her voice on the lawn. She came back in, put the glass of orange juice down on the table and sat down. Her back curved towards Ben showing every vertebra.

"What about Geoff?" said Win. "Shall I tell him tea's ready?"

"No," said Liz. "No thanks."

Amanda opened her mouth to scream. Ben held her chin and filled her mouth up with banana. Beside him Liz was sitting very still, and on each vertebra were grains of sand. Win looked the other way and ran the dish-cloth underneath the cold tap of the sink and wiped the draining board.

In the garden afterwards when Geoff had finished working and Bridget had gone home, the children all been put to bed, Liz wore dark glasses and wore them through until the sun went down.

High up in the attic of Geoff's house, the Hodges lay, with Fiona on a mattress on the floor against the far wall and Amanda in a cot. The sash window was wide open and the sound of the sea came in across the uncarpeted floor and the curtains fluttered.

Win whispered: "Is there anything we can do?"

He had his arm around her: "Do about what?"

"About poor Liz; it's terrible."

He stroked her back. Here on the bed it was dark, but at the far end of the room the moonlight lit the children's faces.

"Did Geoff talk to you?" said Win.

"Not much." He stroked her back and felt her breasts.

"It's awful," Win said.

He moved his hand and she went on talking. "I wouldn't blame her if she left him."

The curtains moved and blew at an angle of forty-five degrees inside the room, stayed there, then dropped down again. Win's voice, whispering spoke of tragedy. "I think it is a tragedy," she said.

Ben's hand in the curve between her diaphragm and hip-bone; he thought of shadows under breasts in summer houses.

"She'll fall for someone else," said Win. "She's bound to, even if it is in spite."

"I love you," Ben said.

"Yes I know," said Win and moved a little nearer him but not quite touching.

As she was lying on her side, the curve of her hip rose under his hand; the hip-bone jutted. Geoff would put a shadow there inside the jutting bone if Win was lying in the summer house.

"I do love you," said Ben.

"And yes, I do know that, but I think you should talk to Geoff, although it may be too late."

If Win was lying in the summer house for Geoff, the colour of her skin on canvas would be paler than the models', pale and frail and pearly like Amanda's; Geoff would paint her pink and gold and her darkest parts would be maroon and smokey brown.

"They used to be so happy. So did we."

"We are happy now," said Ben.

"Are we?"

"Yes, of course we are. *I* thought we were." If Liz was lying in

58

the summer house for Geoff and Liz was painted by him as she must have been quite frequently, her breasts being small would barely flop sideways over shadow. Her nipples very small too, dark and almost to be covered by a teaspoon of banana.

"It's frightening," said Win, "extremely frightening."

"What's frightening?"

"Liz and Geoff."

If Mrs Adderley were lying in the summer house, her breasts would need the darkest, dark green shadows under them. If Joan, his secretary, lay there; firm and round—faint shadow.

"Win—we're happy, aren't we?"

Win murmured and turned on to her stomach so that her bottom was uppermost. Geoff had no pictures of girls on their stomachs with their bottoms uppermost. Ben thought of Win like that and Liz like that and Mrs Adderley and Joan like that.

The patch of moonlight had reached the foot of their bed and highlighted the bumps made by their feet under Liz's cotton counterpane.

He wore blue Marks and Spencers pyjamas piped with white and he stood at the bedroom window looking at the moonpath on the sea; he was leaning out between the moving curtains and hearing the noise of the sea more clearly. His bare feet were on the boarded floor, he felt sand from the beach between his feet and those bare boards.

He went downstairs to the first floor where the lavatory was and, being thoughtful of the noise at night, he did not flush it. He tiptoed to the bathroom across the landing. Geoff and Liz's bedroom door was shut, but their children's door was open. Ben stood still on the landing listening to a long low drawn-in sobbing breath which came from even further down the stairs.

He might have been going down to walk in Geoff and Liz's garden on a fine night when he could not sleep. That, in fact, would have been his justification for the journey had it been demanded. But he went down the bare stairs and into the small hall which had a stained glass door on to the verandah so that the moon picked out the colours which fell blue and red on to his feet.

Liz, who was curled up on the sofa in the living-room in a traditional attitude of despair, did not ask him what he was

59

doing, so there was no need to justify. What she did was to hold out her arms and say: "Oh Ben. Oh Ben."

He was thirty-five that summer; he was five foot ten inches tall and weighed eleven stone. His hair was thinning on the top, and, as Joan Falconer had observed, was neither dark nor fair. He was a reasonably good architect, whatever that means, with ambitions to be a better one and he enjoyed his work. That is to say that, if asked if he enjoyed it, he would say that on the whole he'd rather be an architect than a lot of other things.

He earned £1,000 a year plus a small percentage of the profits of the firm. He paid three hundred a year in interest on his mortgage plus paying off a minimum of £100 of the loan per year. When his mortgage was paid off he would start saving up to build his house, so this would take at least five more years. There could be hitches to this plan; he often worried that he would need a new car too soon, this summer even.

Ben was born in Hampshire, in Southampton. His family were middle-middle class, his father a clerk in a shipping firm with an office at Southampton docks. Ben was bright and went to grammar school. His parents, now retired, had a bungalow in Lyndhurst in the New Forest; they lived quite comfortably; he was their only son and they loved their grandchildren. Win was very nice to them and remembered their birthdays and took the children to see them as often as she could.

Liz saw the moonlight on Ben's feet as he crossed her sitting-room, and in the deeply variable light she saw his eyes without his glasses. He was a good comforter and he stroked her hair and held her hand and said how beautiful she was, because it seemed to him that she needed to know that in her present situation. And anyhow she was, he thought, extremely beautiful.

She was wearing one of Geoff's white shirts and may or may not have had knickers underneath it. Ben did not look but wondered as he lent her a corner of his blue pyjama jacket upon which to wipe her eyes.

Shadows were all around them. "Hold me, hold me just for a second," she whispered, and he did that as chastely as he could.

"You're so good! So special!" she said.

"I'm not. I'm very ordinary," which was a thing he had often

60

said to women and was puzzled when they did not agree, but not unflattered.

Shadows between her neck and the collar of her shirt, the smell of clean hair, another body not explored and not to be explored, the curve of her jaw-bone, cheek in moonlight, everything around them in that room in misty detail.

"You know what this is all about?" said Liz.

"I think so, yes."

"You think it isn't going to happen to you, you think you'll be the one it doesn't happen to."

"You always think that, yes I know."

"It isn't as if Geoff can't have me and always could. I'm not exactly backward in coming forward."

"There there," said Ben and wished that he could focus clearly without spectacles and believing that he looked ridiculous without them.

"I've always thought of you," said Liz "as someone there, if ever . . ."

"Well, I am here."

"Stay here just for a minute, stay . . . just hold me."

"I am holding you." An expression of tenderness on his face was so intense that, had it not been dark, she would have melted even further.

"I'm in deep water, Ben. I'm drowning."

"I know." He rocked her.

"I wish we could stay here for ever like this."

"Sh . . . sh . . . you must go to bed."

"I shan't sleep."

"You will. Now promise me."

"I'd promise you anything, I think."

"Just promise me you'll sleep."

"Oh Ben."

He stayed there after she had gone upstairs, went walking round the room and through the hall, across the verandah, down into the garden, but there there were so many plastic toys with broken edges that he was worried he would cut his feet.

FIVE

"IN THE BEGINNING was the word," the Colonel read at matins the next morning at the lectern of St John's where the huge brass eagle caught the light from stained-glass windows, and his voice went round the Gothic church and into the dusty cobwebbed wooden rafters up towards the belfry.

The beginning of another busy week for those retired. He stepped down from the lectern, stood in the middle of the aisle, turned smartly towards the altar, bowed his head a fraction and resumed his seat. The final words still echoed: ". . . full of grace and truth."

He could not understand how other people of his age found time hung heavy on their hands. He took his hunter watch and timed the Vicar's sermon. He also made some notes with a pencil on the back of an envelope. He noted down the words the Vicar used which, in the opinion of the Colonel were above the heads of all those present; the congregation numbered ten. The words were "ontological", "existential" and "antithesis". Beside this last, the Colonel pencilled "twice".

They shared this vicar; the Grimstones were a plurality. When matins was at St Johns, Great Grimstone, evensong would be at St Michael's, Little Grimstone, and vice versa each alternate Sunday. The Vicar who was young would fold his cassock in the basket of his bicycle and pedal in between the two.

Outside at five past twelve the sun was blazing. The Colonel left the vestry, having counted the collection and stood and gazed down over trees and rooves and gardens. The sun at three days after midsummer was still dead centre of the sky. The flag flew from the flagstaff on the tower; the staff rose up between the battlements.

A busy week ahead: today, old friends to lunch; tomorrow, Monday, a meeting of the County Council Highways; Tuesday, the ruri-decanal conference; Wednesday, Boy Scouts' County

Meeting, and all the lawn to mow; the height of the growing season, this, peak of the year this last fortnight in June when there was Wimbledon, the Second Test at Lords, the strawberries still, the longest day and summer building up in front and people visiting.

The Colonel went down through the tombstones on the side path to the wicket gate which led into his garden. He wore his best grey flannel suit, his bowler hat. He passed the study door, the drawing-room window, and here his wife leaned out, her hair just brushed, a little lipstick on, wearing her best blue-and-white-check cotton frock. "How many, darling?"

"Ten."

"How much in the collection?"

"Eighteen and six."

"Oh well . . ."

"Ontology, antithesis and existential."

"He'll never learn."

In the hall he left his bowler hat and walking stick and stood there in the drawing-room where on the grand piano was a mahogany tray of glasses and two bottles of sherry, one medium, one dry. The sun fell on the garden at the front.

"They'll be here soon," said Mrs Falconer.

"Oh yes. Where's Joan?"

"Oh somewhere, picking strawberries." The mullioned window at the back looked out through fronds of wisteria on to the shady lawn and copper beech.

"Old Pridaux lets him get away with murder at St Michael's."

"Sharing vicars is such a tricky thing," said Mrs Falconer.

The Colonel went in through his study door and put his bowler hat down on a chair. In here he kept his Johnny Walker whisky; he poured himself a large half-glass of this.

Back in the drawing-room his wife was standing by the piano looking out on to the sunny front. "It's awful," she said thoughtfully, "I can't remember which son Dorothy is bringing with her."

The Colonel drank his whisky; the lawn out there, the copper beech, some deck chairs under it in shade.

"There's one called Gavin, I remember; the other Gerald, I think she said was thinking of going into the church. I *think* she's bringing Gerald."

"Old Pridaux," said the Colonel, "has got his mind on other things these days."

"Yes, that's a pity," Mrs Falconer said.

"Civil Defence! I ask you!" said the Colonel.

"I think he rather gets his teeth in things," said Mrs Falconer.

They stood there drinking, waiting. "Yes, I think it's Gerald probably," said Mrs Falconer. The front door of the house was open, likewise the windows, so that the warmth came in and the sounds of bees outside and birds.

"Perhaps we should have asked the Vicar too," said Mrs Falconer, "to lunch I mean."

Along the village street towards them buzzed the Austin Healey Sprite, low slung and white with hood turned back. The childhood friend of Mrs Falconer was driven by her son; they slowed down at the junction, took the left fork up between the houses, cottages and orchards and drew up in the road outside the house.

"How absolutely divine," said Dorothy as her son opened the car door for her to get out. "How too absolutely divine for words." She was hoping to buy a house in Dorset in the near future.

Joan came round the church some time after matins. She saw the Vicar still in his black cassock going down the road to the new rectory, and she waited till he'd gone before going back towards the kitchen garden. From the top she saw the white sports car.

She'd walked for no reason in particular other than it was a dazzling June morning, up from the kitchen garden where she had been picking strawberries, across the paddock where they once kept ponies, up the hill towards the Glebe Land. Here she sat and had a cigarette, hearing the distant sound of the organ and her father's voice, the Vicar's voice and one or two other people singing thinly. It was best to hear it from here on the hill of Glebe field and not to take part in it. Now that she didn't have to go to church and now that she'd clarified her thinking on the matter by telling Mr Hodges that she was an atheist, she quite enjoyed the singing. She smoked a Gold Flake while they sang O Lord and Father of Mankind, her favourite hymn.

The clothes she wore, the old white school aertex shirt and

64

brown corduroy slacks she'd cut off at the knee and hemmed, would do for lunch. There was not time to change; she had done as much for her mother's lunch as anyone could expect from someone on their only whole day off from work. She had picked strawberries, taken them up to the kitchen, gone down for more and left them in a bowl and walked. She went to pick them up now, keeping down well out of sight of the drawing-room window, crouching beside the churchyard boundary wall and climbing in the kitchen window. From the drawing-room her mother's high-pitched social voice. In the kitchen a smell of potatoes baking in the Aga oven, lettuce in the scullery sink. Joan went upstairs and did her hair, her eyes and put some lipstick on.

Dorothy wore a linen suit, high heels, a chiffon scarf, her hair was blue-rinsed and her hand was bony and with rings. "My dear," she said, when Joan shook hands, "last time I heard of you, you were doing awfully well at school."

"She got eleven O levels," said Mrs Falconer. "We were awfully proud."

Gerald wore a blazer with brass buttons, cavalry twill trousers, a shirt open at the neck, silk scarf at collar. Joan shook hands with him and noted well-cut hair, blue eyes, the sort who'd think he was the answer to a maiden's prayer. His mother said to Joan. "I suppose you're off to Oxford in the autumn."

"No, actually . . ."

"Oh Cambridge! Gerald's at the opposition."

"I'm working now," said Joan, taking sherry from her father.

"We hardly ever *see* her," said her mother.

"I've put the rest of the strawberries in the kitchen," Joan said, and heard her mother say how awfully hard she worked, how early in the morning she had to leave and how awfully keen she was on working for this architect.

Joan stood a little back outside the group, one elbow on the piano staring out into the garden. It was her habit at this time to look a little distant as if deep in thought so that even in a non-existent conversation, people might think that here, behind enigma, lurked a personality.

"We would adore to live round here," said Dorothy, spreading butter on the inside of her baked potato.

Mrs Falconer had found a very good way of roasting ham

in the Aga oven and it tasted good; the bread-crumbs had stayed evenly on the outside and she'd added cider for the final hour.

"We passed a simply charming house for sale in Evershot."

"I believe their vicar's awfully good," said Mrs Falconer.

The dining-room, not often used, refectory table, stone floor, huge empty high stone fireplace, sun outside and spots of brightness inside from the gold-leaf on the Derby china. Gerald, sitting next to Joan, said he was going to Greece with a friend from Balliol next Friday. Did Joan know Rhodes at all? And Joan said that she did not know it, but she knew that it existed.

Then Dorothy turned to Joan and said: "I suppose you have heaps of fun down here. There must be lots of young your age. For parties."

"I think I'm rather solitary," Joan said.

"Oh darling, really!" Her mother interrupted, "You know such dozens of people, Joan." She turned to Dorothy. "Joan's got a terrific friend in just the next village. They go everywhere on bicycles."

"How energetic," said Dorothy and she turned and asked the Colonel if the coast was spoilt round here and was it useless to try and settle by the sea. "Gerald," she said "would be lost without a boat."

"Poole's your place, then," said the Colonel.

"But that end of Dorset," Mrs Falconer said, "is really rather different. It's flat."

The Colonel said to Gerald: "So you've changed your mind about the church?"

"Well actually, sir, I wasn't ever too pleased with the idea."

"Quite sensible on the whole," the Colonel said. "Stipends will never keep up with the cost of living. Our man is useless. He is driving away the congregation with existentialism."

There was aerated cider in large tumblers beside every place. Gerald lifted his and held it for a moment just below his nose and moved it slightly as if sniffing the bouquet of wine. This boy, thought Joan, knows the meaning of existentialism but has not talked about it.

"Gerald," said Dorothy, "is thinking of all sorts of things, of journalism or perhaps the Foreign Office if his French is good enough. He's pondering it, aren't you darling?"

"Our vicar," said the Colonel, "would be happiest at Salisbury,

66

following the Bishop, lighting candles, ringing bells, that sort
of thing."

"Oh darling," Mrs Falconer said, "he isn't spiky. Oh no, that
isn't fair."

"Much better be a diplomat," the Colonel said to Gerald,
"That's our only hope." ˙

"Oh do you think so, sir?"

"And that's a dim one."

In the kitchen Mrs Northover, the daily woman, had arrived
and shuffled to the hatch and put the strawberries on it. Joan
moved to fetch them and her chair scraped on the stone floor.

"Strawberries! Gorgeous! And your own of course," said
Dorothy. And in a pause in conversation Joan served them on
to flat white gold-rimmed plates, and spoons cut through them,
echoing on plates, scraping on grains of sprinkled castor sugar.

"And do you think, sir," Gerald said with a strawberry on
his spoon, "and do you think that this new attempt to enrol for
Civil Defence again, could serve a useful purpose?"

The Colonel put more sugar on his strawberries, letting it fall
from the perforated silver ladle, and taking another spoonful,
letting it fall again. He took a mouthful, frowning, chewing fast,
munching, leaning forward looking at his plate. Without looking
up again, he said to Gerald. "No, I don't."

In the sunny patch beneath the window on a wide-seated, soft-
leather chair with arms, the three cats lay intertwined, the ginger
and the tabby and the she-cat tortoise-shell called Moggy. Her
tail hung off the chair and flicked from time to time.

They were all looking at the garden. It was the thing to do after
lunch apparently. Standing in the gravel spaces between the
border where these widened out around the goldfish pond. The
names of flowers were being called out by Mrs Falconer, and
Dorothy was admiring each one, saying she would absolutely
love to have that flower when she had a country garden of her
own.

"Show Gerald the paddock," Mrs Falconer said to Joan.

"Why on earth she should want you to see the paddock," Joan
said, walking on down the path ahead of him, "I can't imagine."

"Horseflesh?" Gerald said.

"We don't have them." She led the way with a walk she hoped

was nonchalant to the very bottom of the garden, to a gate beside the kitchen garden. This gate was ancient, wood split at the joints and rusted hinges, tied to its post and sagging. The sort of gate you did not open but climbed over. "We can look at it from here," she said.

The top bar of the gate on which one would traditionally lean when viewing paddocks, was encrusted with lichen and scraps of rotting wood and bird droppings from the holly tree above. His blazer would have been besmirched, so Gerald stood and lit a cigarette, smoked it through an ebony holder, one suede shoe on the bottom rung of the gate. "How pastoral!" he said. "Yes, very, isn't it? It's rather overdone." He offered her a cigarette. The case was silver and the cigarettes were black, gold tipped and tasted like a mild cigar.

"One does," he said, "rather hope one's mother won't settle too deep into rurality."

"Oh quite," said Joan.

"One can, of course, fill one's vacations pretty well with one thing and another luckily. But, of course, if one likes and is happy with country pursuits, the gun, the horse, the fishing-rod . . .?"

"Well hardly," said Joan, in such a tone that he should realise that she had no truck with things like that.

"What job do you have, if one may ask?" said Gerald.

"Oh just a secretarial thing," said Joan. "One makes the best of it."

"A girl I know had one of those," said Gerald. "Just for the pin money."

"That's all it is, unfortunately," said Joan.

They stood and smoked under the holly tree, looking along the paddock at the ragwort and the burdock and at the slope up at the far end to a clump of trees.

"Of course," he said, "a place like this would have advantages. One could bring one's friends and generally revive."

"One does need that," said Joan, "oh quite."

"And no doubt there *are* other people that one likes. One finds them, doesn't one?"

"Oh yes," said Joan, "but of course one is very committed to one's work." She could see beyond the bursting borders, the heads of his mother and of her mother, moving. Gerald said:

"One rather admires a down-to-earth ambition on the whole. One comes to it in time no doubt."

"It does rather cut out social life," said Joan. "Of course there are parties and the odd Hunt Ball."

"Oh dear," he said. "Does one get involved in all that?" He removed the cigarette from its holder half smoked and stamped it into the gravel at the entrance to the paddock. "It leads to something, does it, this being secretary for an architect?"

"One hopes so," Joan said, feeling as she leaned against the gate, the crumbling gritty lumps against her back and hearing her mother's voice beyond the fluffy heads of flowers.

"On the whole," said Gerald, "though, it's gather one's rose-buds while one may, all things considered these days and all that."

"Oh quite. Oh definitely," said Joan.

"Hiroshima etcetera."

"Oh quite," said Joan. "Exactly rather."

Mrs Falconer stood by the goldfish pond and with one hand pulled absent-mindedly at dead heads on the nearby lupins, scattering lupin pods. "They seem to know exactly what they want these days," she said to Dorothy.

"My dear, I couldn't agree more," said Dorothy.

"We're very fond of this young man she has. His family come from Nottingham, but are really rather jolly people on the whole. They're in some kind of business."

"My dear, so all your birds will soon be flown," said Dorothy and went on talking about her other son, the one called Gavin who had this absolutely enchanting girl-friend who worked in Harrods and whom Dorothy adored.

In the scullery, which was behind the kitchen, which was in turn behind the dining-room, Mrs Northover had the sink brimful of water, grease and potato skins and particles of ham fat floating on the surface; she lifted the plates from the depth of this and put them on the wooden plate rack beside her on the draining board. Joan, after Dorothy had left with Gerald at the wheel of the Austin Healey, stood beside Mrs Northover, dried spoons and forks and put them on a tray.

Her parents put their feet up in the garden, snoozing. Joan went to tea with Richard.

Assume a nuclear attack on Bristol, which was the nearest city to the Grimstones; Mr Pridaux, in this event, would gird himself in lead and test the level of the radiation with some yet undelivered electronic calibrated gauge. And then, if all was clear, he would knock on doors of cottages, houses, farm-houses, manor houses, terraced houses, outlying small holdings, old rectories and new rectories and tell people that they could come out now. It being presumed that the telephones would be out of use and no other means of communication available to the beleaguered population.

"Lead suits would be very heavy," Joan said that afternoon to Richard in the Pridaux garden.

"They will discover something else by then," said Richard.

And, having found the atmosphere now clear of radiation, Mr Pridaux would then connect with Civil Defence Headquarters in the town.

"Where is it?"

"The Conservative Party office at the moment," Richard said.

And having, by previously set-up field telephone, pronounced "All Clear" to HQ, they will connect with Dorchester Control. Control in turn will get in touch with Bristol telling them that anyone who is still alive up there, over there, a little to the north-west, may come here to all the Grimstones and the other villages and towns where the atmosphere is clear and will be clear because of Mr Pridaux's electronic instrument. "It's pretty well worked out," said Richard.

"And has he got the lead suit yet?"

"That will arrive the moment the international situation looks alarming."

They were on the lawn and Mrs Pridaux was coming down the terrace steps with a tea tray. "Just fetch the kettle, Joan dear, will you?"

"Does Dad want tea?" said Richard.

"Not yet, dear. He's working."

"I was explaining to Joan . . . ," said Richard.

"It's far too much for one man to do," said Mrs Pridaux.

"My father said it wasn't any good," said Joan.

"Oh did he, dear? Well naturally not everyone can see . . ."

Jam sandwiches with crusts cut off, jam sponge cake, weak china tea. A magpie on the plum tree, flapping there towards the nesting box. "No leave it, dear," said Mrs Pridaux, touching Richard's arm as he leaned forwards ready to get up to go and fetch the gun.

"Not anyone!" Joan said as quietly as she could, hoping only Richard could hear, "Not anyone with any sense."

"What did you say, dear?" Mrs Pridaux looked at Joan.

"I said I wasn't sure if anyone would take the trouble to do it, you know, like Mr Pridaux's doing it. Because, I mean, most people would be dead, particularly in Bristol if the bomb dropped there and if the wind was in the north-east, then, you see, it would have blown the radiation . . ."

Mrs Pridaux, standing with the teapot in her hand, on the pale and even surface of her weed-free lawn, poured out a cup of tea and said to Richard. "Just take this to your father, dear."

When he had gone she turned to Joan: "You see dear, men need to do things in a time of crisis. It makes them all feel useful."

"But if it's all too late."

"It nearly always is, dear, isn't it?" She held a sugar lump between the silver tongs and looked enquiringly at Joan.

"Yes please."

"It always has been, what men do, too late." She looked towards the windows of the drawing-room where Mr Pridaux sat at the bureau beneath the glass-fronted bookcase, writing letters and arranging meetings for enrolment in his cause.

"There wasn't supposed to be another war," said Joan.

"There always have been wars. There always will be."

"Yes, but this one would be different."

"We can only behave as if it wouldn't be."

Joan drank her tea and took the sandwiches held out towards her. "We have to show the men our confidence," said Mrs Pridaux.

The men were coming out. Mrs Pridaux raised her voice and asked Joan after her mother and her father and her sisters and the people who had come to lunch today.

In the morning Joan looked at Mr Hodges and she said: "In the offices of the Conservative Party just along the street from here, there is the Civil Defence Headquarters now, if war should come."

"I don't wish to know about that, thank you," Mr Hodges said.

"Oh aren't you interested?"

"No. Frightened."

"Most men don't seem to be."

"Well, *thank you* Joan. I must say!"

"I am."

"What?"

"Frightened."

"No you're not."

"I am."

"I only said 'no you're not' to tell you not to be."

"You can't tell people not to feel something that they feel. You can only tell them that it isn't going to happen."

"Well how can I do that?"

"I don't know."

"I can't do that, Joan, can I? Do be sensible."

"So how do people live, knowing what they know about . . . all that . . . Hiroshima etcetera?"

"They live. That's all. Now shall we do some work?"

"That's terrible."

"They work, they take dictation, they draw up boring plans, they work on milking parlours, house extensions, cider stores . . ."

"You mean they carry on regardless?"

"They chew pens, they have their hair permed, bicycle around, are seen in fields with boy-friends at weekends, and, as far as I'm concerned, I've had my war and don't even want to think about another one."

Joan lowered her eyes and opened her shorthand book, lifted her fountain pen to her lips, then lowered that as well. "Does . . . I mean . . . does your wife . . . does Mrs Hodges . . . sort of worry about it?"

"My wife, my Mrs Hodges, Joan, she thinks too much and worries too much in any case. I hope, for God's sake, that she doesn't worry about what you worry about as well."

"I see."

72

"I mean . . . she doesn't worry too much; that's not fair. But she is a thinking person."

"Yes."

"And so are many people thinking people, and assume, I guess, that there is a fifty-fifty chance for all of us, so why not hedge their bets and live as if there is a future?"

"That's a very good idea," said Joan. "I hadn't thought of that."

"And can we do some work now, please."

"I don't see why not."

"All right, then."

"All right."

"All right."

"Can you see anything worth living for?" Joan said not looking up.

"At this moment, yes," he said.

She did look up. Sometimes the sun caught his hair and gave it colours. Sometimes he crossed one leg over the other and one leg of his trousers lifted and you saw his socks and the thin not very hairy leg above the sock. He looked a little healthier today than usual. "Go to the seaside, Joan," he said.

She did go. She was with Richard, fossiling at Charmouth. Rather he was fossiling; she was reading on a rock. And it was raining and she wore her riding mac and yellow sou' wester. To the right the beach curved round towards Lyme Regis. The cliffs were grey and gleaming. Lumps of clay fell off from time to time, stayed wet, then hardened as they dried. Richard, a figure over there, stalking between the sea and the cliffs, hopping between the damp and slippery places, leaning over, moving on in his military cape and khaki beret.

It had been raining, but it stopped. She'd kept her rock quite dry by sitting on it, sat crossed leg with book on knee. Richard beside the sea. The tide was going out. From time to time he stopped, bent down and picked up stones.

Joan ate some chocolate, lit a cigarette and went on reading.

Richard, bending in his woollen knee socks, then squatting in his leather boots; he held a slimy wet stone, rubbed the heavy clay from it and guessed that untold treasure lay inside. He unbuckled the flap of his haversack and fetched his hammer out.

C* 73

She heard the sea which was not rough, but slapping on the shore and heard the sea-gulls. The rain began again and she turned her collar up and pulled the sou' wester well over her face and read.

Richard held the stone; this stone, this large grey stone, as the wet clay casing fell away, this joining of small stones which had been rounded by the sea, was history encapsulated.

In his book they called this stone he'd found, a pudding stone. Or sometimes a conglomerate.

Here on this beach the stones ground down from bigger rocks, were washed for a millenium by the crashing of the waves, and then, who knows, stayed here in close proximity under the cliff. Then clay slumped on to them and stayed there in a dry season, set on them, and when hard, a high tide took the whole conglomerate and rolled it, ground it against other stones, smoothed it, shot it up in a storm on to the shore again where more clay fell on it. And here it is, in Richard's hand, arrived, delivered, selected, having waited for him. Until it broke as Richard hammered at it.

Joan saw the sea; a sense of swell was present. Lyme Regis hidden in the trees, dull green trees under low rain-bearing clouds, Lyme Regis looking closer than it was. Then she saw Richard running, slithering, bag flapping on his side, military cape like birds' wings as he came, his wet face close to hers and in his hands a small grey stone.

"An ammonite, I do believe," he said.

"Oh yes?" said Joan. He held it out towards her, his large forefinger pointing to faint markings, parallel lines of gradually decreasing length which curled themselves in spirals to a centre point.

"Incredible!" he said.

"But I believe in it," said Joan.

He went away again with the ammonite in his fossil bag, hoisting the bag on his shoulder and went towards Lyme Regis. He stared in rock pools as the tide went further out, he chipped at stones; he scraped at muddy clay; it came away in layers, centuries of the history of the earth he scraped away. He did believe one day he'd find the secret of the Universe on Charmouth beach. Evolution, Richard thought, haphazard evolution which ended here, in man, in him, in 1953. This could not be for nothing.

74

"Look Joan," he'd say, when he went back to her, "this cannot be for nothing."

He stood with his boots on soft wet sand, looked out to sea and thought that, if you stood on Charmouth beach and looked out to sea, straight out and not to either side, you could believe it was like this a thousand years ago and still was here unchanged. And something so unchanged would stay unchanged. He stood there, new stone in hand, a stone with other markings on it; tall, straight-shouldered, looking out to sea and breathing deeply, full of cosmic thoughts. "A moment of truth," he'd once heard someone say. "A sacramental moment," he'd learned about at school in English Literature, and this was all to do with love and poetry and important moving earnest things. "Silent on a peak in Darien," someone said. And these were the moments which in love you shared and spoke of in hushed tones and looked into a person's eyes and walked into a sunset having your epiphany.

The clouds were still but must have moved and parted up above his head to make way for a shaft of sunlight, turning the grey sea blue, the grey sand gold. Richard opened his fist; the stone in his hand still damp now glistened all the colours of the rainbow. Moreover there was a pattern on it as it caught the sun.

Now she would understand; now he would show her. Now he would change the expression on her face to wonderment. Here was a leaf, exactly like a leaf but billions of years old. He ran back towards her rock. Panting he squatted down beside her, splashing mud on the pages of her book and told her all he had been thinking.

Joan said: "But just because it's been here all this time, it doesn't mean a thing about the future." She shook her head, lit another cigarette, took another bar of Cadbury's fruit and nut from the pocket of her macintosh and offered him a square.

Chocolate came off the ration in the February of that year and Joan had eaten chocolate daily ever since, Mars Bars and Milky Ways, Crunchies, Aeros, whipped cream walnuts, and still she marvelled that you could see in shops chocolate of all kinds in wrappers piled on counters or behind glass covers or on railway stations or on market stalls, in cafés.

Today she ate and read and went on eating when she'd finished reading. The world of Evelyn Waugh, the world inhabited by

75

people like that Gerald who came to lunch on Sunday.

Now it was Tuesday evening getting towards dusk on Charmouth beach. Joan said to Richard. "There's a fifty-fifty chance."

"Of what?"

"Survival; that's the way to look at it."

"I see."

"Hiroshima etcetera."

"Stop saying that."

"For half the time I will, in that case."

He stood in his shaft of sunlight, which threw his shadow over Joan. "If everyone thought like you, it would be better if the bomb did drop."

There were other people on the beach now. Richard felt like swearing but he never did this in her company. Instead he had some harmless words. When angry he would say "Oh frizzle", and sometimes "Oh Mctavish."

He wished he did not need to make love to Joan. He would not make a move towards that end this evening.

"People in the novels of Evelyn Waugh," Joan said, "would have thought like me."

"They're dead. They always were. They never existed."

"People like them did. Still do."

Brideshead Revisited got rather boring in the end. It was all about religion, dying, last rites, Roman Catholics. Although, thought Joan, if you were going to be religious you might as well go all the way like Roman Catholics. She could understand the Vicar lighting candles sometimes like her father said he did.

"If you are angry with me," she said to Richard on the way home, "but you still want sexual intercourse, you could always think about it as gathering rosebuds, nothing more."

But she said this early on their journey home, long before they parted at the fork, in order that rapprochement could be well established before they said goodnight.

SIX

A GROWING COLDER in July. It started badly, worsening, was raining every day, and then this letter came for Mr Hodges. The envelope was large and square and white; the writing round and flowing. Firm writing where even the capitals had style. On the top left hand corner was the word PERSONAL twice underlined. Joan looked closely at the stamp and saw the postmark over it was Dartmouth; it was posted yesterday and caught the evening post at seven thirty. The envelope lay, white and square in Joan's dark corner of the typist's room on a pile of long manilla business envelopes.

"He's got a personal, then?" Kath said from her table at the window. "Woman's writing?"

"Yes, probably, I think."

"I'm not surprised; he's bound to have a woman somewhere."

"It may not be. It might be from his sister."

"His sister not knowing his home address of course!"

"It's possible."

"Has he got a sister?"

"I don't know. How should I know?"

"You know a bit about him, maybe."

"Not especially."

"Still waters run deep, that's what I say."

"Whose still waters?"

"Yours," said Kath.

Joan opened the other letters and pinned them to their files and piled them in a sheaf. At first she put the white envelope with the postmark Dartmouth on top. Her desk telephone buzzed twice. She put the white envelope at the bottom of the pile. She watched him lift each letter and each file, then turn them face down on the desk and read the next one. And the next. And then he saw the envelope. A short pause while he lifted it and turned it over. Another short pause while he picked it up again and put it down again. Joan looked out of the window, waiting for dictation. From one corner of her eye she saw him pick the letter up again and put it in the pocket of his jacket.

"His wound," said Kath when Joan came back, "it doesn't seem to hamper him a lot."

"I don't know what you mean."

"His love life going on in spite of it?"

Kath giggled all the morning, telling everyone who came in, excepting Mr Puller. They all had girls, she said, girl-friends somewhere, all the men. Men were like that, Joan should learn, but cowards if they got found out. Her Dad had had a thing for years with a woman in a pub in Weymouth. Her mum flailed him when she caught him out. It happened all the time.

Joan said to Richard in a field that night: "Do you think your father was continually faithful to your mother?"

"Yes of course."

"But do you *know*?"

"No, of course I don't; I just assume he was."

"And do you think that, if he had, it would have been with several other women?"

"I don't know, Joan. I don't know. Maybe he was tempted sometimes . . ."

"And do you think . . ."

He lay beside her on the grass, but not directly on the grass. His military cape was spread; the night was cool.

"Most books have adultery in them somewhere," Joan said, lying in the darkness with a moon above the trees.

"Like this," said Richard.

"This is fornication, not adultery."

The trees were dry-leaved now and rustling and in the next field cows were stirring. Joan said: "Your father had a wound. Where was it?"

"In his chest."

They made love then. A rabbit squealed. They kept their heavy sweaters on throughout and heard the last bus coming up the hill. There was the usual smell of grass and cows and something dead smelt sweet which might have been a shrew nearby or something larger like a rabbit several hundred yards away. Trees in the night against a moonlit sky look dead, have lost

78

their green. The peak of summer's past, thought Joan.

A rabbit squealed again; there still were traps around that caught the rabbit in a set of iron and jagged teeth and held it there until it died, or until a man came in the morning, prized the teeth apart and knocked the rabbit on that special place behind the head. In a year or so this would not happen any more because of myxomatosis which was on its way at that time from Australia, where Richard often thought of going on cold evenings like this.

Richard and Joan held hands. Since early on in their relationship they had decided that post-coital tenderness was most important. And Richard stuck to this and never leaped up and said "let's go" for at least five minutes, which was considerate for an energetic young man. Joan would have lain there all night usually. Because it was easier to lie than to get up, to be warm in the shelter of the hedge than to stand up in the breeze, easier to lie here than to walk on the tussocky bumpy field where grass in the dark was silvery and cold.

She lay post-coitally and thought of Mr Hodges; since he was such a boring-looking person, even though extremely nice, it was unlikely that more than one other woman could be interested.

"What are you thinking about?" said Richard.

"Oh nothing much."

"Perhaps we ought to go away."

"Perhaps we ought."

"I mean go right away."

"You mean Australia again?"

"Well *somewhere*."

"Oh I see."

He stood up, standing in the dark above her: "You sounded keen last time we talked about Australia."

"That must have been when I was reading *A Town Like Alice*."

"You don't think seriously much," he said.

"I do think seriously."

"Not like other people."

She lay in the shelter of the hedge and said: "How can you tell how seriously other people think?" and watched him walk away out of the shelter of the tree and stand on a tussock in the moonlight, then come back. "Nothing to stop you going to

79

Australia," she said, thinking how sorry Mr Hodges would be for her when he heard that Richard had deserted her for Sydney or the outback. "I'm not stopping you."

"We are in love."

"We are, we are."

"I might go somewhere anyway." He was silhouetted and the lower, outer branches of the tree were just above his head.

Joan sat up. "What do you mean?"

"You know. I might have chosen wrong." He looked up at the sky as if considering each moving cloud which passed across the firmament as having relevance. "I sometimes think that life goes past here rather."

"You're right," said Joan, "it does," and lay back down again. He went on standing, head against the sky, a noble profile really.

"I couldn't go and leave you here."

"Why not?"

"Because I wouldn't."

Their bicycles were propped inside the five-barred gate out of sight of the road. This gate opened easily; Richard lifted the iron latch and swung it back into the field. Joan wheeled her bicycle out; he followed, propped his bicycle against the bank and closed the gate. They pushed their bikes on up the hill towards the fork. They stopped again; his hand was over her hand on her handle-bars; his hand felt cold; her legs and feet felt cold. The church clock of Great Grimstone struck eleven and the sound of it was wafted unevenly towards them. Also carried in the wind, and in the distance, the church clock of Little Grimstone struck. Richard said: "Do you think we'd quarrel much if we were married?"

"I don't suppose so," Joan said, "not more than lots of people."

"It shouldn't be like that. It shouldn't be just not more than lots of people; it should be never."

"Oh well; perhaps we wouldn't."

They were in the village, riding slowly along the street where a few cottages still had lights on. The whirr of their wheels and dynamos and a single barking dog. Their front lights shone round patches which wobbled on the road in front of them.

"Don't you want to be a solicitor after all?" asked Joan.

"It doesn't seem important always, that's the trouble."

80

"Your mother would say you should have thought of that before."

"I don't think she would now somehow."

Tall plants like hollyhocks and sunflowers were shadowed in the cottage gardens. Hedges and shrubs where lights were on behind them, showed in dark shapes across the road.

"After all," said Richard, "in business, exporting is doing something for your country."

"It's also doing something for yourself," said Joan, but afterwards, some time later, she, considering this conversation, decided that very few people had jobs which could be called entirely selfless.

They turned left into the road which led to the Old Rectory and the church. They had passed the pub in darkness at the junction. Here was a single street light, but the sycamore tree beside it blew, flapping leaves across it, making changing shapes on their hands and faces as they went below it. Richard said: "It's nice to think that you think it might work for us."

"I suppose I do," said Joan.

"I mean it wouldn't be such a disaster if something happened."

"Such as what?"

"I mean, say, if you got pregnant or something terrible like that."

"I can't get pregnant; we've never done it without a thing."

"I know, but wouldn't it be nice one day if we could do it properly?"

"It *is* properly. There's no question of it not being properly."

They stopped by the side drive of the Old Rectory. The building stretched away from them and the narrow lawn between it and the road was black except for a patch of light at the far end thrown out from Mrs Falconer's bedroom. At the opening to the drive were lilac trees, their blossoms dead and heavy. Richard and Joan stood under these and had their goodnight kiss. "I'll miss you tonight," he said.

"I'll miss you too."

"We didn't really quarrel, did we?"

"No, not really."

"I *love* you."

"I love *you*."

"I'd better go now."

81

"Yes, it's late."

"I do love you."

"And me you too."

"And will you think about the other thing?"

"What other thing?"

"My future. Ours too really."

"Yes of course."

He mounted his bicycle with a leap as if elated. He wobbled down the village street, turning to wave from time to time, and at the junction disappeared. She pushed her bicycle up the drive and left it against the garage wall, went round by the garden and through the kitchen door, the kitchen, along the stone-flagged passage to her father's study door. She opened this; the Colonel was in the swivel chair at his desk; his lamp, his anglepoise was shining on his papers and his glass of whisky.

"Hello little one."

"Hello Daddy."

"Have you had a nice time, wherever you have been?"

"Yes thank you."

"Your mother's gone to bed as usual."

"Oh goodnight then."

She went along the hall and up the oak stairs, her hand on panels she had felt with this left hand ever since she could remember. She had lived here always; the Colonel was not one to take his family on postings once there were so many of them.

"Hello darling," said her mother from the four-poster bed where the cats lay tucked around her feet.

"Hello Mummy."

"And have you had a lovely time?"

Mrs Falconer ate cereal at night in bed. A bowl of Weetabix was on her knees. "We had another letter from Eve today."

"Is she all right?"

"Oh yes; she's awfully busy with the baby, though."

"She always is."

"Yes, I suppose she always is. Anne's pregnant too."

"She always is as well. Oh by the way . . ."

"Yes, darling?" Mrs Falconer was reading. Like Joan, she read a lot of Neville Shute. She turned the page of *Pied Piper*.

"Is the water hot?" said Joan.

"Oh yes I think so, darling. Take the cats down will you."

The tabby and the ginger and the tortoise-shell; Moggy was the eldest. "I think she's pregnant," Mrs Falconer said, "so leave her here."

Joan carried a cat under each arm. Downstairs in the drawing-room, she opened the casement window and dropped them out; they would claw their way back up the wisteria to her mother's room.

The bath in the Old Rectory was the same as it had been since it was put in. A fifty-year-old bath, it stood on legs and jutted out from the wall like a bed might in a bedroom. The floor was cracked linoleum, the walls were tiled half way up with patterned tiles. Above that there was blue square-patterned wallpaper, peeling off in places.

Joan lay under a cloud of steam, disparaging the bathroom and her body. The body was all right for Richard, but no one else would want to see it. Her breasts were ordinary, her legs too fat at the top and her ankles not up to the standard of a model. Joan dreamed of a bathroom which she would achieve one day, where perfectly proportioned, in a bubble bath, and with plants and books and shining white walls, she'd lie receiving visitors.

At school some girls had pale pink nipples on the end, where else, of mountainous breasts, veined and looking as though they were already full of milk. They flopped embarrassingly in changing-rooms and bathrooms. The girls with tiny pointed breasts could move around like boys, no flopping. And when there were measles in the school or ringworm or chicken pox, they stood in rows while Matron looked for spots on the floppy and the pointed and the rare round upturned standard perfect type.

You could change your bathroom, but you could not change your body much. Even if you gave up eating chocolate, your ankles would stay as imperfect as your breasts. And there was no way she could think of, easily to change her bathroom.

"I hope Liz is all right," Win said that evening.

"Oh yes," said Ben at supper time.

"Well do you think she is?"

"I hope she is."

Then after supper Win was in the garden, hoeing the lines between the peas and beans, moving the hoe more frantically than was necessary. She stopped sometimes and looked up at the windows of the house.

And later as Richard rode home below Grimstone Hill in moonlight, Ben decided that in just such a high place he would build his house. He was in his drawing-office; in front of him, pinned to his sloping drawing-chest, the ground-floor plan. Beside him on the table was the square white envelope that came to his office in the morning post.

Before taking up his pencil he covered the envelope with a rolled-up plan, but the plan rolled off the envelope, exposing it to the eyes of anyone who might come in, so he lifted the drawing-chest from the table and slid the envelope underneath it so that only a triangle of white stuck out to remind him not to leave it there indefinitely.

He sat in the high white room with black curtains drawn across the window. Traffic noises from outside and a little south wind moving the sash of the window. Ben on his high stool in his shirt sleeves, ruling lines on paper, making the shape of the rooms, neat black delineations shaped his future dining-room, small quarter arcs where windows opened, more arcs for doors; a door into the hall and one into the kitchen.

He sat up, stretched and put the pencil behind his ear and reached for the letter underneath the chest. The envelope was already open and he only had to slide the letter out, stiff white paper, like the envelope and covered in this same clear royal blue writing. He unfolded it:

"Dear Ben. You will have opened this in the office and thought what, for heavens sake, is she writing to me here for? And you're right to ask. I hardly know myself. I only know that that Saturday was the turning point for me, and what I want to say might be misunderstood by Win."

He put the letter on the house plan and leaned his elbows either side of it, adjusted his glasses and read on:

"And to think we nearly put you off because of all our agonies (no—my agonies, not Geoff's—his pleasures). Your visit (and Win's of course) was therapeutic definitely.

"I think I can hang on here. At least I think that as I write,

84

because a word to you, a word from you if possible, makes me feel a little loved again. A *little* loved, please note, because I know that's all I have a right to ask from you."

The low-hanging light above the table moved on its flex in a slight draft from the window. It shone on Ben's bald patch but there was no one there to see it.

"Oh Ben, what can I say, except that there we were together in this miserable house and that you were nice to me? I've always known that, were it not for Geoff and Win, there would have been a deeper link between us. I think you've known it too."

The letter lay across the rectangle marked Lounge with one corner spreading over Hall just by the front door which, in an arc, opened outwards on to Paved Area. The site, when chosen, must command a vista such that, when Win opened her front door or looked out of her downstairs windows, all of south-west Dorset would be spread before her.

"Or are you everywoman's comforter? And, even if you are, it makes no difference. There was always something, *that* I know, but listen to me . . ."

A hill somewhere above the Grimstones, beyond the clump where Richard ran, and higher still, so that, when she stood on the paved area, Win would see the sea.

"But listen to me, Ben, (it even gives relief to write your name), you need do nothing; think of me and even write to me; and, if perchance, perhaps, per-anything, you might be driving west (or north or east or anywhere) and there was the remotest chance, well, here I am. Don't contact me here—I know that sounds ironic after all Geoff's done . . . but where I can be contacted . . ."

The land must fall away from where Win stood. A lawn and shrubs in front, a path down to whatever country lane, a flat bit at the side with grass for Fiona and Amanda, first on tricycles and then on bicycles.

"I have a friend called Rosemary in all my secrets. You could write there or ring. A lady of complete discretion."

Ben folded the letter, put it back in the envelope and slid the envelope back under his drawing-chest. He picked up a block of blank paper and began with his pen to write: "Dear Liz . . ." Then tore the sheet from the block and screwed it up.

Upstairs were padding footsteps and Amanda crying.

He looked at the ground-floor plan in front of him. This house must be as neat and light and airy and convenient and pretty and unusual as any house that Win had ever seen. It must have depth of colour too, contrasting cosiness as well as brightness, and Win must say "oh yes" and "what a good idea" to everything.

He sucked his pen; then found he'd bitten it, reminding him of pens Joan used, all chewed and dribbled on. Horrified, he threw it in the waste-paper basket along with the letter he'd started to Liz.

Joan, still considering physical perfection in the bath, decided that it might be best to be the sort of person Mrs Pridaux liked; to be both awfully nice and sensible like Sally. Or better still to be those things and be sophisticated as well.

That writing on that letter Mr Hodges had this morning was sophisticated writing. The writing on that envelope was round and firm, had style. It was from someone with a finished personality, who might be clever, beautiful and awfully nice and with experience of life. With everything.

The Colonel walked along the passage, banged the bathroom door and called out; "Get a move on in there."

"All right," called Joan. "All right." She was enumerating her experience of life. She knew the lanes of Dorset and some parts of London and of Salisbury where she'd been to school, and a bit of Paris where her second sister lived. She'd been to Scotland once. She knew the Kings of England and the plays of Shakespeare, the poems of John Keats, a little Tennyson, most of Waugh and D. H. Lawrence. And D. H. Lawrence lived near Nottingham, which brought her back momentarily to Richard.

She knew well logarithms, trigonometry and Pitman's shorthand. A smattering of T. S. Eliot. She was able to mend a puncture quickly. She knew the operation—the make/break circuit of an electric bell and roughly how a wireless worked. She knew the numbers and references of all the files at work and could lay her hand on any in a hurry. She knew the way he turned his head as she came in, the way he took his handkerchief out of his pocket and rubbed the lenses of his glasses with it.

SEVEN

"Is RICHARD'S MOTHER all right?" Mrs Falconer once asked Joan.

"Oh yes, I think so . . . Why?"

"She sometimes looks exhausted and I can't think why. She has a daily woman every day and only a smallish garden."

"I think she had an operation a few years ago."

"Oh did she? Hysterectomy?"

"No one said."

Mrs Pridaux, you could say, walked half the speed of Mrs Falconer. When gardening, she did it carefully, kneeling on a sponge rubber mat to protect her bony knees. When going upstairs you sometimes saw her stand at the turn in the stairs and seem to be looking for dust on the banisters. And she never went upstairs unless there was no one else to fetch her what she needed. But she went to meetings like Mrs Falconer did; to the Women's Institute and Mothers' Union and was on a committee in Dorchester to do with orphaned children. She did things that people's mothers did in those days and still do. She had a gin and tonic regularly at six before she got the evening meal and another while she cooked, one later after dinner always.

"I wonder just how rich they are," said Mrs Falconer.

"They've only got two children," said the Colonel.

"I can't remember what the business is or was," said Mrs Falconer.

"Wire nippers," said the Colonel.

Wire nippers brought the Pridaux useful things like central heating and the cocktail trolley. They had a thermos bowl for ice and the earliest kind of food-mixer available in this country. They did not have a television set but only because they said they would not like it; the programmes were not good enough, they said. They had two cars, the Humber which Mr Pridaux drove

88

and Mrs Pridaux's smaller Morris Minor. Richard said his father never had an overdraft but always an account in credit. It must be odd, thought Joan, to have a bank statement from which to spend each month. Her own was usually sent with 10–6d. in the red.

There was always whisky, gin, martini, sherry, and not only on the trolley. There was a cellar at Green Pastures. Mr Pridaux bought cases of whisky rather than bottles. Once the Falconers went to drinks and Mr Pridaux brought a new bottle up from the cellar when the Colonel had finished the one on the trolley.

"What are they like?" Joan asked Richard.

"What are what like?"

"Wire nippers."

"Just wire nippers."

"Aren't they special?"

"They are industrial," said Richard.

"How do you mean?"

"They're sold to factories, to people who make wire and so on, firms who use wire in manufacturing."

Somewhere in Nottingham the nippers piled in stockrooms, warehouses, in boxes, crates and were moved by forklift trucks to other warehouses and railway stations for dispatch. The Pridaux when at table sometimes talked about Dispatch, but seldom about the goods dispatched. If Richard had gone into the business, he would have started at the bottom, in Dispatch. He would then have moved to Sales. And, if Richard had gone into the business, they sometimes said, then there were expansion plans, for export. But, as Mrs Pridaux said to Joan: "His father's heart went out of it rather. And then the take-over, of course . . ."

Joan asked Richard: "Who took them over?"

"Mansfield Metals."

"Could you still work for Mansfield Metals, if you changed your mind?"

"I suppose so. Why?"

"Just wondered."

"A man," said Mrs Pridaux, "needs to have his heart in something. That's why, since Richard's heart seemed set on something else, we all decided . . ."

The married Pridaux daughter, Sally, came home sometimes. Her husband, Johnny, was in marketing in Mansfield Metals.

He came less often but the once Joan met him he came in a fast low car with Sally with a white headscarf round her head. They held hands, having not been married long. Joan came into the Pridaux drawing-room and saw them looking out of the window, Johnny's hand on Sally's bottom. Joan went out again, embarrassed.

A deteriorating July, but within the fortnight's span of rain and drizzle and hardly ever lifting clouds from hill tops, came this morning, bright, but too bright, sky far too blue over deep and soggy green.

The Pridaux garden early in the morning; Friday and the Pridaux's daily woman just arriving on her bicycle, Richard having left for work, his father having gone off in the car to start the day aright discussing fall-out in another village. And Mrs Pridaux on the terrace.

The Pridaux terrace swept each day, no growth between the crazy paving stones, but just around the edge, a little sedum, a fleshy and insinuating plant, had crept in this damp weather and sent its tendrils towards the centre point where the Pridaux garden parasol was fixed on a steel post screwed and bolted every early summer into a purpose-made and permanent round slot. And Mrs Pridaux sitting under this beside the wrought-iron table. And with a great deal on her mind.

The first thing on her mind was Richard; he wasn't studying enough. Last night he'd promised to stay in and then he'd asked if he could borrow her car and take Joan for a drive.

"Oh dear," said Mrs Pridaux, "I thought you would be studying."

"I've done an hour," said Richard. "An hour at least and I promised Joan . . ."

"I am sure she'd understand . . ."

"The car would make a change for her."

"She seems to like her bicycle."

Last night at midnight, Mrs Pridaux sat in bed and heard him coming in. She sat up in bed; her teeth were not beside her in a glass, but in her mouth. Her teeth were her extravagance, and a rare one; at forty she had had them capped or crowned. And there they were in evidence when she smiled.

The second thing that on this summer morning, where the

sharpness of the shadows was somehow troubling in itself, the second thing that bothered Mrs Pridaux was her husband. He rushed at things; like Richard, Mr Pridaux went head down, throttle out. At sixty-two he still went furiously at things and was inevitably disappointed. His energy and eagerness might summon up support, but such support would depend entirely on his continued interest and would wane the moment that waned. Unless, thought Mrs Pridaux, an international situation loomed.

The Pridaux lawn below her, horse-shoe shaped, mown short, the edges trimmed, carnations bending towards the centre turning sugar pink. Beyond this, shrubs with silver leaves; behind all this the compost heap in brick surround and out of sight. The sun had been up several hours and so the steaming out of foliage had taken place.

The third thing on her mind, and this was much more on her mind for much more of that morning and that day and month and year and always than either of the other two was Sally, Mrs Pridaux's daughter. A pain this was, a real and deep and nagging anxious pain. And, unlike the other worries, there was nothing she could do but wait. A letter not arriving on a Friday; two Fridays letters not arriving.

Between the silver shrubs and the beech hedge and beside the compost heap, there were the fruit trees, young apple, plum and cherry, new enough to have their metal name tabs still fixed on, tender enough to be protected from the magpies, one of which now twittered, but Mrs Pridaux did not even look around to see if the rifle was in place. Worse still, a jay with brown and blue and bright white plumage, could just be seen within the branches of the plum tree where the nesting box was fixed.

Three things on Mrs Pridaux's mind, and on either side of her in white painted wooden tubs two matching miniature conifers with tops grown level with the parasol and shaped to keep their outline every spring with shears. Their shadows marked a further symmetry.

The first thing on her mind : this could be shared with Mr Pridaux; of Richard they talked endlessly at night, of his career, his aptitude for it, of whether it had been wise to let him choose it.

Four things on Mrs Pridaux's mind : if Richard didn't study because of Joan, where would that get him? It might get him

Joan. A flimsy cloud came out from behind the house and dimmed the sun and Mrs Pridaux shivered on the terrace. The jay flew up away against a darkening sky.

Five things on Mrs Pridaux's mind: if there was something wrong between Sally and her husband, this threatened Mansfield Metals also, and thus became a further threat to Mr Pridaux's peace of mind.

Six things on Mrs Pridaux's mind; so many things on Mrs Pridaux's mind this morning while she watched the magpie, almost wishing for another because, although not superstitious in the slightest, that would make two for joy instead of one for sorrow.

The sun that morning also shone extremely brightly on the pavement of the street when Joan and Richard, having cycled down together, went their separate ways and leaned their bicycles against the buildings where they worked.

On the windows of the downstairs room where Richard worked was large gilt lettering. This spelt out: Critchell, Hansen, Hansen, Solicitors and Commissioners of Oaths. When the sun came round full south these letters would throw shadows on his desk.

He yawned in the dusty sunshine; then he stretched; he would be studying through lunch today; he'd just told Joan he would not see her till this evening.

An articled clerk who aimed to become a fully qualified solicitor had to pass at that time two parts of the Law Society Exam. The whole process for non-graduates must take at least five years. Richard took part I three years ago. Part II he planned to take last year, but was not ready.

The sun shone in and on to the volume open on his desk entitled *National Parks and Access to the Countryside Act, 1949.*

The other clerk, a man of Richard's age, was off on holiday. This made it easier to work and think because this boy was always talking. And Richard used both desks for all the other books and maps and papers that he needed for this task.

If Richard's heart had been in Law in 1950 as Mrs Pridaux had suggested, it was not in it now. He'd worked all yesterday on Hambury Parish Council versus Collett and it looked like it would take all day today as well. He moved to lift the window open, wedged it with a rubber wedge; a breeze came in; the map

92

of Hambury Parish on his desk, the flimsy 1:25000 blew away, the page of *Access to the Countryside* flapped over and his notes were scattered.

"Frizzle and Mctavish," Richard said.

He went to the dusty bookcase in the corner, fetched some small but heavy books and weighted down the map, the *Act* and started work again.

Outside were voices, people walking, running, shopping, cars were passing. The thing on Richard's mind that morning was to find out whether Collett had the right to put a notice saying "Private" on the public footpath when it ran through his farm.

"It all depends," he said last night to Joan in his mother's car, "it all depends if it's a footpath or a Green Lane."

"It could be just a track."

"You don't have tracks in law," said Richard. "You only have Green Lanes or footpaths."

"How ridiculous," said Joan.

In *Access to the Countryside,* as Richard read this morning in the office, there was a paragraph which said that Green Lanes were not subject to repairs by local councils, but nowhere did it say that "Private" notices could be placed on them.

Richard did not smoke, nor eat sweets; there was nothing pleasure-giving to bring distraction to these books, these papers or these notes. He stood behind the lettering of the window, looking out. Slowly moving sideways, his face, which had been just behind the word of Oaths, was now behind Commissioners, then Hansen, Hansen; finally he stopped behind the Critchell. Although for Richard, all these words were back to front and mirror writing.

Mrs Falconer dived into the garden at about this time to weed the long herbaceous border. The Colonel stood on the lawn and watched her kneeling, weeds and earth flying through the air as she tossed them in the vague direction of the wooden basket. He looked at the thermometer in the shade outside his study door. He went inside and tapped on the banjo-shaped barometer which hung beside his desk. The needle moved to Change. He opened his diary and wrote down: "Change. Temp. 69 Fahrenheit." Then he read the letters which had come this morning.

Another one from Eve in New England about the baby, from

Anne in France about her pregnancy and a letter from his bank manager telling him his overdraft had reached above the limit set and would the Colonel visit and discuss this, please.

A bill from Cunard White Star for their crossing from Southampton to New York in four weeks' time for the christening of Eve's new baby. The Colonel bent down and opened a lower drawer in his desk; he took a file of share certificates and wrote a letter to his stockbroker.

Above him on the desk-top, three photographs of Eve and Anne and Hope. The photograph of Joan was elsewhere, her presence in the flesh each evening was sufficient.

He had one daughter married to an Englishman. Hope married Jeremy who lived in Chelsea and was connected with a Merchant Bank. Although the Colonel was not given to summing up his life's work or his family's achievements, Hope had done best so far, it might be said. When Hope gave birth at least a visit to the christening only cost the fare to Waterloo.

By lunch time it was cool; clouds gradually assembled; they came up from the west and covered all of Dorset, bringing unpleasant weather for the weekend just beginning. People went on doing what they had been doing, excepting Mrs Pridaux who gave her husband lunch and listened to what he'd been doing all the morning and watched him tick the names on lists he'd visited and heard him say that so and so was interested and so and so was not.

He noticed that she was not eating and expressed concern.

"I wish you would not worry, dear," said Mrs Pridaux, "Tell me how the meetings went again."

He paused and then began again.

But Joan ate lunch alone, and in the café where she ate, she felt much stared at by people who would think: "What's happened to her boy-friend?"

At least she was herself with Richard. At least she kept to the ethic she'd been brought up with of intellectual honesty. At least she told him what she thought. And that was how things should be, wasn't it? Between two people, wasn't it? And good looks and intelligence were enough, they said, apart from Mrs Pridaux.

"Above all to yourself be true," Polonius said in Hamlet in the speech they learned at school by heart.

But being true meant also being rude. She stared ahead ignoring all imagined stares. And being true was difficult when you were shy of telling someone like Mr Hodges what you'd tell him if you were completely true unto yourself.

Intelligence was very over-rated when it did not give you answers to all this.

EIGHT

BEN'S OFFICE WINDOWS rattled and the sky outside was grey.
A depression, so the wireless said this morning, had moved into
the Atlantic and was sending winds of gale force up the south
coast. In the dark, Joan sat opposite him in winter clothes, tight
skirt and high-heeled shoes, black stockings, sweater, almost-
orange lipstick.

The sea had lashed the Cornish coast and then the Devon coast
and when he drove Fiona to the pebble beach on Sunday afternoon the waves were breaking on the piers and salty green spray
hit their faces.

"I see you've decided summer's over," he said to Joan.

"Yup. That's right."

Unsettled weather in July. Across the road the windows of the
Swan Hotel were shut and low clouds raced eastward above its
roof. Joan was a dark presence under the map against the off-
white wall.

"Did you have a nice weekend, Joan?"

"It depends what you mean by nice."

"All right, I wish I hadn't asked."

The draught from the window flapped at an unpinned corner
of the map, the south-west corner by Lyme Regis; the wind
whistled under the gap beneath the door into the passage. Joan
crossed her legs and waited with her shorthand notebook.

"How's young Richard, then?"

"He's not that young. He's twenty. . . ."

"All right then. Letters."

On Saturday morning he worked in his drawing-office at home,
continuing the house plan. Then at lunch time, because Win
seemed quiet and tearful, he said "Let's all go shopping", and
they drove to Dorchester and struggled round the market in the
wind. Win said she'd like to buy some clothes, so he held the
children while she tried on cotton frocks in crowded shops.

The people in the street wore transparent plastic macintoshes which blew and flapped in other people's faces, and Win found nothing that she liked.

"Dear Mr Atkinson . . ."

"Dear who . . .?"

"Dear Mr Atkinson . . ."

"Oh, the cider store man . . ."

"The same . . ."

They drove back from Dorchester against the wind. They stayed in the house, the children sat on the table in the back-room looking out on the rain they'd driven through. Ben worked in the drawing-office in the evening until Win came in and said they must make friends round here or buy a television set, however much it cost them. Then she went to bed.

"Dear Mr Atkinson. With reference to my recent visit to your farm . . . and to your cider store in process of erection . . ."

Joan bent her head and made her outlines.

". . . it is my opinion . . ."

Sunday was worse; Amanda had a cold and would not eat. Win sat with her on her knee all afternoon and Ben put Fiona in the car and drove. At the harbour they stood on the west pier and watched the waves, narrowed to force their way between the wooden piles, pass up towards the harbour and pass up again.

". . . that the fault in the timber we inspected will not finally affect . . ."

In the harbour where the waves surged up, boats rocked and sea splashed on to cars parked round the edge. And then another wave before the boats had settled, then another. Ben clutched Fiona against him in her red macintosh and red wellingtons, and looked at other people bent in the wind against each other and wondered what they did at home on Sundays.

"However . . . I will be in touch with Briden's Timber Mer-chants and arrange a meeting at the site . . ."

When Ben got home on Sunday afternoon Win said that they must make some friends or buy a television set or he must join a club so that they got to know more people. She was in the kitchen reading the *Sunday Times*, leaning against the draining board while Amanda ran water in the sink and splashed Win's feet.

"I look forward to meeting Briden's representatives and your good self later in the week . . ."

"Your what?"

"Your good self."

"Do you want to say that?"

"Yes, I said it."

She sighed, recrossed her legs and wrote.

"Now that's the lot. Now get them typed up please."

She stood up. "Yes."

"Stop sulking, Joan."

"I wasn't sulking."

"Yes you were and I won't have it."

She stood in the doorway, very reddened mouth trembling.

"Get on with it and shut the door."

Ben put his feet up on his desk, his swivel chair pushed back and lit his pipe. He looked at his shoes, the rattling window and the flapping map, the picture of Fiona and Amanda on his desk, the pile of paper in the In Tray, and the Out Tray which Joan should have emptied. His raincoat on the door still moved where Joan had shut the door. The ceiling of this room, as noted often, was too low.

And yesterday Win said they must have friends and said they might ask Geoff and Liz to stay for the weekend. "All right," said Ben, "let's talk about it in the morning."

This morning Win was still asleep. He got up rather early.

Ben thumped the metal desk and lifted up the telephone. He pressed the button opposite Joan's name.

She came back slowly, standing in the doorway.

"Now listen Joan . . . sit down."

She walked to chair, sat down, head bent, shorthand notebook open.

"I'm not dictating letters to you, but I am dictating to you. Just stop this sulky thing. I will not have it. You're a smashing girl and *don't* you know it? I don't know what's happened to you this weekend, but I've had a bloody awful time and I'm not taking a bloody awful sulky time from you. So just get up off your bottom and get on with it. That's all."

As slowly as she had sat down she stood again and closed her shorthand notebook. Ben at the desk put his head in his hands and thumped his fist again. "I'm going out now."

98

"I see."

"Ask Kath to check the letters through with you and you can sign them."

"Yes."

"All right then?"

"Yes."

"No hard feelings?"

"No."

"All right then."

"Yes."

"And no more sulking."

"No."

"Chin up. That's right."

"That's right."

"And off you go. And take the Out Tray with you. Do what you're told and everything will be all right."

Joan went along the passage and down the stairs, the Out Tray balanced on one arm, one hand on the banisters to steady herself. She stopped; the stairs curved down towards the well. The light was from a skylight, domed above her head. She stood quite still and watched the clouds go past above the skylight.

Chin up. A little up was how she held it, and she held the Out Tray with one edge on her hip, delicately she held it, jutting out from her hip-bone, head held high she descended to the first floor, preparing for re-entry to the typists' room.

She opened the door, glided in and sat down at her typewriter. From her handbag on the desk beside her she took a cigarette and lit it, puffed at it, watched the smoke curl up. He needed her to take his orders.

"What did Hodgekin want, then?"

"Nothing much."

"A waste of time your going then?"

"Oh not at all. Oh not at all." Joan gazed past Kath out of the window.

"Oh! She's been struck by lightning, she has!"

"If that's what you like to think," said Joan, picking up quarto headed paper, carbons, thin copy paper, lining them up so that they would travel through the carriage of the typewriter with precision.

"It doesn't strike twice, thank the Lord," said Kath.

These letters would be perfect with no rubbing out, no changing of the words; these letters would be spaced and centred on the page. No typed word would extend beyond the margin of the heading. They would be visually impeccable. For your good self; that would stay. For your good self.

Yesterday he said to Win. "It's just a matter of getting through the weekend."

"But it shouldn't be."

"I think it is."

"It's as if you're saying grin and bear it."

"Well I am."

"It's as if you're saying it's not worth trying to improve things."

"No I'm not saying that."

She sat with Amanda on her knee, both small, both thin, both ready to be swept away in any storm. He knelt on the floor beside them, took a hand of each. Amanda snatched hers away and Win's stayed apathetically in his. "Oh hell," he said.

He walked within the four walls of his house, came back into the back room. They still sat there. He looked out of the window. "Is there anything particularly . . .?"

"Particularly what?"

"Well worrying you or anything?"

"What do you think could be worrying me?"

"God knows. I don't."

The trouble about Win was that she once had been a cipher clerk. She was in the Admiralty. Then she'd gone on to decoding for Intelligence. And had been good at that as well. You never knew with Win. She was that much sharper than he was and never left a thing unfinished. She didn't look like that. She looked the way he loved her. That is to say, the way she looked he loved, and it was hard to believe that, behind the freckles and the grin and the occasional atmosphere of frailty, there was a ticking mind, a watching eye, a calculating person.

He'd called her kitten once.

He moved around the room and watched them sitting. "At least you have each other," he said.

"What are you talking about, Ben?"

"You and Amanda; you have each other."

"Oh thanks a lot! You take her. Do!"

"Come on, kitten," he held out his arms towards Amanda. Win stayed quiet; she'd probably remembered that he'd called her kitten once.

He held the baby and the handkerchief which went with her and jogged her round the room. "It's only passing," he said to Win.

"What's only passing?"

"This, all this." He gestured to the room, the rain outside, the gloomy sky. "Why, what did you think I meant?" He gave Amanda back to Win and took Fiona to the stormy sea instead.

The sea was grey and green and the troughs between the waves enormous as they rolled towards the harbour piers and crashed. Ben, facing east with the wind blowing his hair in strands in that direction, Fiona clutched in front of him. To his right, to the south of him, had he turned his face that way, the tops of waves as far as you could see were white. Spume blew off their tops and into the sky which was in such weather indistinguishable from the sea. The sun was somewhere. He stood half way along the west pier of the harbour entrance in his fawn raincoat with Fiona, in her bright red hood and cape and wellingtons, and watched the waves sweeping up the harbour.

He could buy a television set. It would mean that, if the Hillman gave out now, this year, this summer, he'd be pushed to buy another car. Some people said you could get cars as part of salaries, but he'd have to wait until Puller and Son became Puller and Hodges. But bother that; he'd buy a television set. They'd missed the Coronation, but he'd buy a television set. He decided that on Monday. He was driving at the time along some complicated lanes towards the Grimstones.

Joan had this fountain pen, a Parker 51. She sat under the map, and when he stopped dictating, she would put it in her mouth, the end of it, purple pen in red mouth, and sucked. Sometimes he could hear her sucking it, and sometimes the sucking action made the ink blob out the other end. So that when he did start dictating once again, there would be bright blue Parker Quink on her shorthand pad, her fingers and her skirt. He told her not to suck the pen, not to put its smooth round end between her lips.

101

Today she had black stockings on. For once they were not snagged, but when she crossed or recrossed her legs, he saw, just below her knee, a blob of nail varnish where she had stopped a ladder running.

He had meant to buy a television set this lunch time but he'd have to do it on the way home; on hire purchase, he supposed. You could, of course, make love on Sunday afternoons if you put the children in their room and locked the door. Or had a television set and left them watching that downstairs. If there were programmes on Sunday afternoons.

He would look in Dr Spock and see if there was any harm to children watching television while on Sunday afternoons their parents went to bed. It must be happening all the time, Ben thought, while driving through the windy lanes.

"I wonder," Win said yesterday, "if you'd feel differently about her, if she was a boy."

"About whom?" Ben asked.

"About Amanda. Who did you think I meant?"

He was driving on high ground and holding the wheel as a skipper steers a ship in a storm. But up here was where his house should be, but his house would be close to a village and a pub, a shop, a school. You could not build in complete safety. Fall-out, as Joan reminded him, would come. And, even when she didn't remind him, just looking at her sometimes brought forebodings of a cataclysmic nature.

Down in the valley, Bottle Cottage missed the gale, but on this grey day, it was like night inside. Mrs Adderley's shape against the tiny kitchen window blotted light out. Ben at the table drinking coffee, his plans in front of him.

"You look tired," said Mrs Adderley.

"I thought you'd like to know that we could manage to make the doorway into the extension larger, here. Look here." Her hands on the table and her bosom level with his chin. "Here," he said, "another foot, say, on the width. The wheel chair . . ." He could hear her breathing, and, out of the corner of his eye, he could see her breasts rising and falling and feel her looking at his face and not his plans.

"But I thought," she said, "the plans had already been submitted to the County Council . . ."

"Yes, I know, but I had this idea, you see . . ."

"It's marvellously good of you to bother with us . . ."

"It struck me that negotiating the chair through a gap which was only just wide enough . . ."

She came round the table and leaned beside him, her fat upper arms touching the material of his jacket.

"I thought," said Ben, "I ought to remeasure the width of Mr Adderley's wheel chair . . ."

She pointed her finger to the place in question on the plan; her wrist watch on elasticated metal chain nestled in flesh; no bones were visible. "I see," she said, "I thought we had."

"What?"

"Measured it."

This room had even lower ceilings than his office. She coughed and the cough vibrated through the table; her finger jerked a half-inch across the paper of the plan. Ben felt into his pockets for a pencil, reached into the depths of his brief-case. He marked with two faint lines the place on the wall where the opening could be extended.

"Let's measure it again," she said.

Mr Adderley sat in his wheel chair half way down the lawn outside the cottage. The wheels had made lines on the grass where Mrs Adderley had pushed it this morning. Mr Adderley's legs were covered with a tartan rug and his white hair lifted in the breeze. There were no flowers here. Just grass, short grass, then longer grass at the edge and a stone wall as a boundary. The orchard was beyond the lawn, the hills around reached up to meet the low grey sky. A sun-dial in the middle of the lawn.

"My word, it's peaceful here," said Ben.

On the lawn no sound as they walked, nothing echoing from the treeless hills around. Beyond the lawn, the apple trees, leaves flapping, flashing undersides, the unripe fruit bobbing.

"Too peaceful?" said Mrs Adderley.

"Oh no. I didn't mean that. It's very . . . soothing. Yes, it's soothing."

She put her hands around the sun-dial top, not quite circling it. Her bulk shielded it from any sun there might have been to tell the time. "You are looking for your place," said Mrs Adderley.

103

"Oh rather. Yes. I always am," said Ben, referring to his building site.

"Your special place."

Ben folded his arms, looked at the sky and sniffed the grassy smell.

"I see you as a valley person."

"Well, actually," he took the metal measure from his raincoat pocket and shifted it from hand to hand.

"A wood and valley person."

"I don't know . . . I was thinking more . . ." He pulled the calibrated metal strip and let it go to spring back tightly closed again.

"A heartland person." Mrs Adderley was looking hard at him, a searching look.

"Oh really?" Ben said looking at the sky where birds were sliding sideways in a wind you could not feel down here. He let the measure snap again. "A heartland person?" He buttoned up his raincoat.

"I hope you find it," said Mrs Adderley beside the sun-dial. Her brown dirndl skirt was laced at the waist, her peasant blouse laced at the bosom; the laces dropped and mingled, vaguely dividing Mrs Adderley in two. "I hope you find it."

"What?"

"Your place. Your special place."

In his fantasies she bathed him, fondled him and lay his head between her breasts. In reality she embarrassed him, in fantasy embraced.

What Win would like, he sometimes thought, and thought again as he drove away from Bottle Cottage, what Win would like was a list of his infidelities and where they'd taken place. As follows:

Mrs Adderley, twice in orchard with Mr Adderley watching from the wheel chair.

Joan Falconer daily at ten on office floor.

Liz endlessly and everywhere.

His previous secretary, once in the car and three times in her flat.

Various clients on various extension building sites.

Some farmers' wives in barns.

A woman at a conference in Birmingham.

The last one, being factual, he would of course exclude.

The Hillman took the climb up from the Adderley's with difficulty, clutch slipping and tyres slithering on the track. At the top he turned along the flat road, nearer than at Bottle Cottage to the clouds. He slowed to let a bright green bus come past.

The pub he stopped at was on this same straight road, exposed and blown upon so that the Huntsman's Ales sign swung in its metal bracket, squeaking. The wind lifted Ben's raincoat and slammed the Hillman door shut. In the bar, blank faces of farm labourers, stone flags and scrubbed bar counter. Ben was stared at while he drank his pint of light ale, sitting on a wooden bench.

He had two more calls to make and, with luck, they'd take him all the afternoon. He would still be home early with a television set for Win.

Close study of the map under which Joan sat to take dictation would reveal that Ben's first call that afternoon would take him towards the edge of the county almost into Somerset; his second call would take him in a straight line back towards the middle of the county, north of Dorchester. At four o'clock he took a slow way home through narrow lanes. The gale increased and every lane was full of leaves and twigs torn down and branches hanging.

A wagon loaded high with hay brushed the topmost hedge of the deepest cut of this lane. It came out of a gully and met the wind; swathes of hay were blown on to the road, then slid up against the lane-sides and blew against the Hillman windows.

A bit further on, a tree was down. A tractor was there, two men with a saw and chains to put around the tree trunk; cars piled up in a queue and some turned round and took another route. Ben waited, smoking, with his window slightly open. On the back seat, files from his visits flapped and carbon copies of letters typed by Joan blew loose. He waited there for half an hour while first they sawed off branches from the trunk. Then the tree trunk creaked against the chains, the tractor engine roared, men shouted and waved their arms and other men stood round and watched.

"While you were out," Joan typed in black capitals underlined with red. "The following occurred . . .

11.05 hours. Your wife rang.

12.15 „ She rang again.

2 p.m. (I mean 14.00 hours) Mr Atkinson (cider) rang.

2.30. Your wife again.

2.43. precisely. Mr Atkinson rang again. Since now he mentioned the urgency of the matter, I tried to get you at Mrs Adderley's, but she said you'd gone. I knew you'd taken the Perrot Farm file, so I rang you there. No luck. Then Stokesby Brothers. Once more you had moved on.

3.15. Mr Atkinson wants to see you urgently. Top of cider store about to collapse seemingly. Or seemingly about to collapse. Or looking wonky anyway.

3.30. Wind abated slightly.

4.00. Ran round to Osmond Builders where you sometimes go. No luck.

16.30. hours. Got fed up of trying.

16.45. A woman rang from a call box and would not leave a name.

5.00. Went home, leaving this for you. Plus 'Personal' letter which came by second post (unopened). Correction: did not go home; am going to pictures.

MESSAGE ENDS.

"Oh very funny!" Ben said aloud and screwed this paper up in the empty building at five forty-five.

NINE

AT HALF PAST six Win stood at the bathroom window looking out between the yellow curtains. With the children in the bath behind her she looked down at the garden. The lime tree upper branches bent towards the town, the sand from the sand-pit flicked up and settled and the space beside the garage where Ben parked the car was empty.

"Where's Daddy, Mummy?"

"He's gone to see a man about a cider store," said Win. "He telephoned." She took the pink face flannel which was Fiona's and soaped it and washed Fiona, then the blue face flannel which was Amanda's, washed her, wrapped her in a large blue towel and held her on her lap. Win sat on a cork-topped stool in the bathroom and rested her head on the top of Amanda's because it was somewhere to put her head.

"Why is your head like that, Mummy?" said Fiona from the bath.

She carried Amanda still wrapped in the towel across the landing into the front bedroom. Cars were passing westward, and across the road the cows were in the water meadow, sitting because of rain to come. From a drawer she found a nappy and a pair of plastic pants and began to dress Amanda whose legs kicked in the air as she lay across the small bed which was Fiona's.

There were two thoughts here, thought Win. The first thought was that, from what the secretary had said on the phone, Ben *did* have to go to Axminster.

The nappy pin was missing. Win crossed the landing back into the bathroom, took it out of the nappy which Amanda had been wearing and went back to the bedroom where Amanda was running naked by the window.

Thought two was that he could combine this with another visit.

She caught Amanda, pinned the nappy on, pulled on the plastic pants and found the top of her pyjamas, the blue ones with pink rabbits on them, fought to get the arms in sleeves.

Thought three (this extra) was that, because of the potential dual purpose of the journey, she might never know if the combination had been made.

She forced Amanda's legs into pyjama trousers, sat her up, watched as she threw herself away and rolled across the bed and staggered on the floor towards the window shouting, "Daddy, Daddy."

Thought four (another extra) was that she would know nothing until he returned. And even then she might not know.

She caught Amanda and put her in the cot, which began to rock and rattle and bang against the wall. Amanda pounded with her feet on the mattress, clawed at the cross bars, yelled and threw the blankets on the floor and yelled again.

Thought five; that it was all hypothetical anyway.

Back in the bathroom Win said she was going to count to twenty and then Fiona must get out. Fiona said: "No thirty, please."

Thought six was that the hypothetical was as painful for the thinking woman as the factual. She wrapped Fiona in the big pink towel. "Why has your face changed, Mummy?"

Thought seven was no longer thought but hate and anger. And she rubbed Fiona, rubbed her everywhere, her hair and back and threw pyjamas over her head, pink ones with blue rabbits on them with elastic at the wrists and ankles. Thought eight was anger and revenge, thought nine was blurring tears.

She stormed across the landing, opened the bedroom door, went to Amanda who still stood screaming and flung her flat on her back, forced her legs down, tucked the blankets in and slammed the door. An expression appeared on Amanda's face, a hitherto unknown expression, which was one of astonishment. Inasmuch as an eighteen-month-old can register surprise, Amanda, you could say, did look astounded.

Thought was resumed, but less numerically. Downstairs Fiona in the back-room armchair, eating an apple in pyjamas, listening to a story. Win's voice kept steady as she read and the sky outside became a darker grey.

Hypothesis was suspicion, Win thought grimly, reading by the garish light outside where the grass seemed to be reflected in the sky. She cleared her throat and made her voice ring out.

Suspicion needed grounds. The evidence was this: the letter, still sticking out beneath his drawing-chest. Postmark Dartmouth. Untouched, unread, even though your hands and fingers, when in its vicinity, twitched with the urge to open, read and tear in half.

Fiona curled in the armchair with an apple in her hand and listened.

The evidence, part two: Ben's weekend restlessness.

The lime tree sharp against the sky, the window rattling, Win reading, the clothes line stretched, the clothes prop bobbing with no clothes on the line. The line, a white thin cord which caught the light.

The evidence continued: alternative explanation for Ben's weekend restlessness; the weather, lowering barometric pressure, her own depression (cyclic, although also caused by lowering barometric pressure). Moreover, Ben's mood often echoed hers.

Fiona sitting bolt upright with apple core in hand and asking why the story ended there, too early, well before the end. "Some stories do," said Win.

Some other evidence: that time at Liz's house when he got back into bed and lay there very still. And further: looks exchanged next day.

"What time is Daddy coming home?" Fiona asked.

"Eight forty-five I'd say," said Win. These calculations had taken place:

5.45, he would have left for Axminster.

6.30 (at the latest), he would have arrived at Atkinson's.

6.45, Commence inspection of the cider store.

7.30 (hypothetical), Conclude inspection and have drink with farmer, possibly. (This based on his description of a previous visit.)

8. p.m. (hopefully), leave for home.

8.45, reach home, and if reach home, what happiness!

"What is eight forty-five?" asked Fiona.

"Quarter to nine," Win said and pointed on the clock to where the big hand would be at that time and to where the little hand would be.

She closed the book she had been reading to Fiona and asked herself three questions:

1. Is it true that suspicion in the long run creates that which is suspected?
2. Would thinking people think that seriously?
3. Is it better to have loved and lost than just to sit around feeling jealous all the time?

"Just like a man," said Mrs Pridaux, lifting up the oatmeal woven cushion and finding Mr Pridaux's spectacles for him.

"Well thank you, dear," he said. "Where's Richard?"

"He's gone to the cinema with Joan."

Mrs Pridaux put on her own spectacles and sat down opposite him and began to knit a beige wool sock for Richard. Mr Pridaux opened the *Daily Telegraph* at the financial page. "She seems a jolly girl."

"Oh do you think so, dear?"

"I suppose that means you don't," he said from behind the paper.

"I didn't say that."

"No?"

She knitted fast, holding the knitting towards the lamp, into the pool of light, although it was still light outside, but blowing spats of rain against the leaded diamond window panes. Her long legs were crossed at the ankles and she leaned back sometimes, held the knitting at arm's length. Mr Pridaux put down the open *Daily Telegraph* across his knee. "What is it then?"

"What is what, dear?"

"You'd better tell me."

"There is nothing wrong."

"But you *think* there is?"

"I didn't say that."

Mr Pridaux got up from his chair, folding the *Daily Telegraph* as he moved towards the cocktail trolley. From the lower cupboard he fetched the Gordon's gin and a bottle of tonic water. They had had drinks before their dinner. He mixed a gin for her and took a whisky for himself, whisky with ice from the thermos bowl and water from a jug. "Is it . . . is it . . . Johnny?"

"Inevitably."

110

"Is there a letter?"

"Yes of course."

"From Sally? One that I can see?"

"No dear. I'd rather not."

"Ah."

"It came as no surprise. Last time we saw her, I did wonder . . ."

"But she said nothing then."

"I didn't think she would at that stage."

"I saw her only ten days or so ago . . . she didn't look too happy, but . . ."

"You didn't want to worry me . . ."

"Exactly."

They sat on either side of the fire-place, each with a small round drop-leaf table. On his was his tumbler full of whisky, ice and water, on hers a gin and tonic. At their feet was the black and fawn woven rug. The polished fire-irons in the grate glanced in the light of the lamp by which Mrs Pridaux did her knitting.

He said: "Is there anything we can do. Should we go to her?"

"No dear, definitely not. At this stage."

He lifted his glass to his lips and stared out at the rain: "Poor old Sal."

"Yes."

"Poor little Sal."

"It just depends if she can cope with it."

"And have you told her to?"

"I don't know what you mean, dear. One cannot tell her at her age."

"She listens to you."

"Oh, do you think so?"

"A good thing there's no family. That's a bit of advice she took from you . . . to wait . . ."

"I said a year at least and she's been married three."

He put his whisky down. He stood up, went towards the window, carefully drew together the short beige curtains, sliding them along the white painted window sill and blotting out the wet night and the china ornaments and photographs. "Funny about our children . . ."

"What do you find amusing?"

"Odd. I mean. We did everything."

She nodded, picking up her knitting. "Yes, I think we did."

"It's up to them now."

"One can only tell them that."

He was a man with plenty of hair for sixty-two, brushed neatly over a well-proportioned head. He wore a fawn cardigan with a cream shirt open at the neck and had sandals on his feet. He had eyes of a fairly penetrating blue which neither of his children had inherited, but his regular features had passed on to Richard.

"Is it a little girl?" said Mr Pridaux.

"Is *what* a little girl?"

"The trouble . . . Johnny's pecadillo?"

"He's on the road a lot, you know. It happens."

"*Yes* dear."

"I don't need to remind you."

"*No* dear."

"Poor Sal. She's not as strong as you."

"In fact I think she is, but we shall see."

"It's all a bit of a jolt," said Mr Pridaux. "Quite a shock."

And Mrs Pridaux said: "Not really dear."

She had never liked surprises. Even for her birthday and for Christmas she would make out lists of what she needed rather than be surprised and have to act spontaneously in pleasure.

The only thing he'd ever seen surprise her once was a daisy on the lawn when all the other daisies had been systematically destroyed with selective daisy killer. One day last summer she bent down and said: "My goodness me! A daisy dear, in spite of all your treatment!"

At nine Win sat in the back-room with the wireless on, volume low so that she could hear the children if they woke up and hear Ben's car when it drove up.

The wind combined with the music which was of broad deep harmonies, symphonic, grand and tragic and she turned it off. She stood up to do the ironing, ironed his blue shirt and sat down again in the red armchair.

Outside before it got dark, the swing was swinging in the wind, but then she drew the curtains. Now there was rain, drops hitting the window pane. The weather forecast said the depression was finally moving up country; soon it would be breaking over South-ampton, rocking liners, over Portsmouth, rocking warships. Hail over Winchester and Salisbury Plain.

Down on the camp site by the harbour, someone said in the shops today to Win, a caravan had been blown over, a child's leg broken, family gone back to Sutton, Surrey with an unfinished ten days of their fortnight. Storm cones had been hoisted all along the south coast. At the bad weather watch at Liz and Geoff's house who knows what damage would have been done to Geoff's nude ladies?

The tree uprooted earlier, where Ben waited, now sat there massively beside the road, its remaining branches pointing to the sky, its shape intruding into the lane's driving space, outlined with red lamps; County Council warning notices up and down the road. At Bottle Cottage there would be just wind and dark-ness in between the hills where Mrs Adderley would have the wireless on. Or else she would read out loud to Mr Adderley and worry about the apple crop.

Monday in those days was still traditionally washing day. All over, and in most cases unassisted by twin-tubs or automatic front loaders, people who had not heard of tumble-driers, hung their washing on the line like Win did today and saw it blow horizontally across back gardens, raised free of the ground by clothes-prop poles. Clothes pegs came with gypsies to the door; flapping shirts then rolled and left a little damp were now being ironed, or left unironed like Ben's grey and his khaki on the ironing-board.

Win curled in the chair, as small as Fiona, taking as much space as Fiona did two hours ago. She held some reading matter without reading it: Ben's magazine, *The Architectural Review*.

Above the Hodges' house, up a road behind it on a hill, the cottage hospital lights stayed on all night; the labour ward's high windows, naturally unnaturally bright, where a woman Win saw in the shop today was giving birth, womb four fingers open, so the midwife said, so don't press down yet, dear; I said don't press down. But have a whiff of this and yes I'll ring your husband and say how well you're doing. Whispers in the corner. "It will be four hours yet at least, I'd say, so don't ring Dr Beanie. Let him sleep." She took her metal trumpet and listened to the baby's heart inside the stiff round mound on which the navel stretched open to its limit. The woman, known to Win as Sylvia, moaned; the pain began again. She'd read the book by Dr Grantly Dick-Read and practised natural childbirth by herself because there was no local clinic yet for such aspirations. She breathed and panted, but stomach muscles pulled against the breath; the pain was like this; it was like this; no, it grew and was like this; trees falling, roots as they come mauling through clay, disrupting life underground, beetles, worms disturbed came hurtling out, sharp tap-roots dragged and wrenched and savaged. The secateurs which Mrs Falconer used to dead-head roses, red hot, white hot Pridaux wire nippers.

Win covered her face with Ben's *Architectural Review*.

Women who knit like Mrs Pridaux or drink gin each evening, who, like Mrs Pridaux nod over life and swallow anger, jealousy and grief, and smiling blandly at their husbands, move gently in their drawing-rooms, puff up the cushions before they turn out the light, and, even as they bend they feel that funny pain again they've had before.

In the hall Win stood and listened up the stairs; she raised the telephone receiver, heard the dialling tone and put it down again. She was in the drawing-office, circling his working table. She saw the letter still protruding; she pulled it out, looked at the postmark Dartmouth and pushed it underneath again.

At half past ten she gripped the drawing-office table and watched the hairs on her arm stand out as if drawn by some magnetising influence. The hairs on her head felt stretched and pulled out likewise, roots tearing like the trees and dying as they tore and going grey.

"Oh God," she said instead of screaming.

Her mother had a nervous breakdown once and underwent electric shock treatment and was fairly all right afterwards.

Grey hairs at the age of thirty-two, thought Win. Take to a rinse out of a bottle, take to a hairdresser the rinse gone wrong, take to another salon every month and have the roots touched up. Forget the colour that your hair once was, get crow's-feet round your eyes which people will call laugh lines, signs of real maturity.

At the same age as Win's mother had a nervous breakdown, Ben's mother became a Roman Catholic quite suddenly.

In the hall there was just the telephone, still the same telephone, the same table and the wooden chair beside it. Still the same Win in flowery belted dress, the same legs and arms she'd always had.

Up at the hospital where the legs were now strapped up and wide apart, the woman Sylvia whom Win just knew, said: "I'll never go through this again." Wearing masks, they switched the flood-lights on her gaping labia major. "They all say that," the midwife said, "but you'll come back. The birth rate will rise for years to come." The focus of interest was not the woman Sylvia, but the stretched blue tunnel and the head of another female person approaching but still at least another hour away.

Win on the hall chair, head in arms on knees. She rocked and mouthed: "He must ring soon, he must come back soon, he will ring soon, he will come back soon."

The film finished and the titles rolled. They stood at attention for God Save the Queen and saw the new shot of the Trooping of the Colour where the Queen rode side-saddle head up as in the portrait of her by Annigoni. Richard let Joan's hand drop for the National Anthem and stood to sharp attention.

Joan thought of ways of getting to look like Ava Gardner. Richard at attention leaned fractionally forward, raising his heels from the cinema floor which was, in any case, a sloping floor. He said that this was how soldiers on parade were told to stand; it stopped them fainting.

In East Street they met the rain and wind head on and cycled into it. If you held your chin up, just for a stretch, you could be Ava Gardner in the bows of the Flying Dutchman's galleon, braving the elements with your fine eyes and your smudgeless lipstick.

Ben got out of the car and stood in the gale by a telephone box. He felt in his pocket for the letter with the number on it. Who was this Rosemary he had to ring?

Why was he in this telephone kiosk? The heavy door blew shut after him; the kiosk smelt inside of vomit and stale cigarettes. He could not find the letter. He leaned against the shelf and felt for change in his trouser pocket. He looked at his watch; it was ten o'clock precisely. "It is ten o'clock precisely," Ben said, as the woman voice of TIM would say if you were in London

115

and could dial that code. But it was ten o'clock precisely in the market square of Axminster in Devon, where the fish and chip shop on the corner was just closing. Ben pressed Button A.

"Oh that's you, is it, Win?"

"Well, who did you think it was?"

" Your voice sounds funny, Win; you sounded just like someone else."

She sounded even more like someone else when she said: "Who did I sound like?"

"You see, I'm drunk," said Ben.

"I noticed."

"But I love you. Don't be someone else. I'm going to buy you a television set. I love you; I've been drinking Mr Atkinson's scrumpy. The cider store still stands."

'Well, that's all right then."

"Is it? Good. Your voice sounds awfully funny, Win. I'm coming home."

Mrs Pridaux went upstairs and Mr Pridaux went out to check that the greenhouse door was shut and to shine his torch on his tomato plants, the leaves of which had earlier shown signs of magnesium deficiency.

The Colonel walked around downstairs; he shut his study door and had a final whisky.

Mrs Falconer was reading *A Town Like Alice* between mouthfuls of Rice Krispies. She got out of bed to shut the window from which the rose-patterned curtains were blowing wildly in her direction. She tripped over the cat. "Oh bugger you," she said. And put her hand in front of her mouth in horror, picking up the cat to stroke it, saying: "There there Moggy Moggy there there Moggy. There there Mummy didn't mean it."

116

TEN

TOWARDS THE END of July the front of the Old Rectory was covered with climbing roses with dead heads, with wisteria which had flowered and fallen, and japonica, a spiky shrub. At one end there was the yellow honeysuckle and on the southern sunny wall, the red Virginia creeper rising to the roof.

In the front border tobacco plant and stocks and cat-mint grew and tangled with themselves either side of the garden path, and in the kitchen garden way out at the back of the house beyond the lawn and other long herbaceous borders, the soft fruit cage was full of raspberries. Mrs Falconer picked them once a day and Joan went down there in the evenings and ate as many as she picked into the old enamel saucepan.

The soft fruit cage was so old now that the sides drooped inwards and many of the wooden cross-beams which were meant to hold up the wire-netting roof, had broken, split and hung down catching at your hair. Blackbirds got in and flapped around and could not find the holes by which they'd entered. Imprisoned birds; Joan crouched down and dreaded flapping wings. The cage was now untended and the raspberries rampant; the gardener came once a week but concentrated on potatoes.

You came up from the raspberry cage between the back herbaceous borders, under the pergola and across the lawn towards the kitchen door, your legs scratched, your clothes torn and with red stains on them. The border plants, which were not staked, fell forwards on the path, Canterbury bells and phlox, gypsophila, gaillardia and white and yellow giant daisies had to be stepped over. You would have thought that everything that was going to flower this summer would have flowered. But still things went on coming out. The Colonel and Mrs Falconer were going to New England in a few weeks' time, but would be back in time for the Michaelmas daisies and chrysanthemums.

And Mrs Falconer about this time became of a mind to have

a party of some kind. She looked at Joan and realised that some social responsibility towards this youngest child was unfulfilled. That Joan had never had a coming out. Well, she didn't want one, but all the same one must do something for the young. One always did. Even if Joan was different. The Colonel said it was not a matter of difference but a matter of stupidity. No, Joan was not stupid, said Mrs Falconer. Remember the eleven O levels; Joan was not stupid, not at all. Joan was at a shy and gawky age all girls went through. The Colonel said that all he knew was that she was at a bloody awful age.

It would in the end, Mrs Falconer decided, be a tennis party.

"But I don't play tennis," said Joan.

"Of course you do," her mother said.

There was a tennis court beyond the kitchen garden. In the war they grew potatoes on it, but the new young Vicar who came in 1946 and moved into the new young rectory (built 1938) with young children, got up a working party, returfed the tennis court and used it for the Youth Club. It wasn't the sort of game the Grimstone boys took to much, and if the boys didn't like it, the girls would not be bothered either. So the Vicar and his wife played on it themselves mostly in the evenings. You could hear them from the raspberry cage, their voices discussing their children and theology between the serves and strikes.

"No one *ever* has a tennis party now," said Joan.

"Of course they do," said Mrs Falconer.

"So who do we ask?"

"Well, Richard, of course, for a start, and the Vicar and his wife."

"Oh big deal!"

"Don't be silly, darling."

There were plenty of people who played tennis after all. If all those tennis parties had gone on before the war, there must be people who still played. Not everyone was dead or wounded. Mrs Falconer wanted lots of young to come. "The Vallances," she said, "they've lots of young."

"They're all away," said Joan.

"Young Giles Vallance; you used to be quite keen on him."

"He's absolutely awful. He's incredibly stuck up."

"Oh dear. I always thought he was a nice boy on the whole. He will be down from University by now."

But Mrs Vallance on the telephone said Giles was spending July and August with a friend in the Dordogne.

They went through names of other young whom Joan had met at parties in the past few years and none of these were still at home; they'd all gone off to University or abroad or to be au-pair girls or got jobs in London. "Oh dear," said Mrs Falconer, "well there's definitely Richard and the Vicar and his wife."

There was also Sally, who had come home two weeks before and whom hardly anyone had seen. She spent her time sun-bathing on the lawn at Green Pastures in dark glasses, or in the spare-room, Richard said, and did not want to talk about the reason for her visit. She cried a lot, he knew, but his mother would not have her questioned. "Poor old Sal," said Richard.

"How dreadful for her," Joan said. "What happened?"

"Something pretty dreadful," Richard said.

"Don't you know?"

"No, not exactly."

"Haven't you asked?"

"One doesn't, does one?"

"Why doesn't one? It can't stay secret always."

"I guess . . . I guess that Johnny took up with another woman."

"It happens, doesn't it? Why all the fuss? She'll find some-one else."

The Vicar mowed the tennis court and rolled it, pushing the mower and then the roller out of the new rectory drive and into the old rectory drive one evening. He was not very young, but still quite strong at thirty, muscular and blond and red-faced. The Colonel said that Joan must help him so she emptied grass over the hedge into the kitchen garden each time the bin of the motor mower filled with short green cuttings.

"Not seen you in church lately," said the Vicar.

"Oh sorry," said Joan, "I have a lie-in on Sundays. I work most Saturday mornings."

"You career girls!" said the Vicar.

"I have to earn my living."

"Don't we all? You like the job, though?"

"Not particularly; it's a job." Joan in her green skirt sat on the bit he had mown and leaned against the post which held the tennis net, folded her feet in sandals under her skirt. The Vicar had golden curly hair but his red face spoiled his looks; he

119

would be fat soon. These big blond men like Richard went off disappointingly.

"I'm looking forward to it ever so," the Vicar said.

"To what?"

"The tennis party."

"Oh that!"

His trousers bulged as he sat facing her with his legs apart and leaned against the boundary netting; his balls must be enormous. Joan swept remnant grass cuttings with her hand across the grass and made a pile of them around the netting post. Birds squawked from the raspberry cage.

"The Tremletts want to come," said Mrs Falconer.

"Who?"

"Arthur and Averil Tremlett. You know, darling. They are awfully nice."

"Oh, I know who you mean."

"And Averil's frightfully keen on tennis."

"Is she?"

"She nearly played at Wimbledon before the war; they may not be young, but they're the next best thing."

The kitchen garden, through which guests would have to walk, was bursting with lettuce gone to seed, shot three foot high, and onion flowers; cucumbers romped from the frame and were fat and round and unlike cucumbers; the asparagus bed was like a miniature fir forest, and out of the broken green-house windows, a fig tree burgeoned and an old vine forced its way. The Colonel worked there, cutting, scything, and the gardener on his Wednesday hacked at the hawthorn hedge.

"The players will be Averil Tremlett, the Vicar and Mrs Vicar (I never know whether she wants me to call her by her christian name or not), the Pridaux, Richard, Sally and Mr—I suppose we ought to call him Harry, and yourself; that's seven."

"I'm not playing, am I?"

"Oh darling, yes of course you are. I'll tell you what; I've thought of someone else. Another young."

"Oh who?"

"That man you work for . . . Mr Hodges."

"Him? He's not young; he can hardly walk, let alone play tennis."

"Mr Pridaux was wounded on the Somme and he plays."

"Not in the thigh. I'm sure Mr Hodges wouldn't want to come."

"I'm sure he would. They're new round here and probably would be extremely touched to be invited."

"You mean you'd ask his *wife* as well?"

"Well, yes of course I would. *You* ask them."

"I can't possibly."

"Why on earth not?"

There was a stream running past one end of the tennis court, a sludgy small brook which went into the river further down. The court was raised and a steep bank fell towards the stream, where kingcups grew in spring and white irises. But in July it was muddy, full of roots and frogs and possibly water snakes. Joan had to cut the bank with shears.

"She couldn't leave the children," Joan said.

"Who?"

"Mrs Hodges. She couldn't come because of the children."

"Well . . . she could always bring them with her. I think that would be rather fun. You ask them."

"No." Joan pushed shorn grass down into the stream . . . "All right," she said, "I might."

"I don't know what you think about sometimes, Joan."

"Does anyone?"

On the Sunday evening Joan looked at the stream from where she sat, having sheared the bank above it. She used to go down there in wellingtons and catch newts and tadpoles. She reached and stirred the muddy bottom with the rusty shear-blades and sighed for lost childhood pleasures.

Ben wrote to Liz: "I got your letters and I tried to ring your friend one evening. Would have done more but you know how it is by our age. By God, we all know how it is by our age, don't we? You do need help but I'm not sure I'm the one to give it. That is sad. The night I tried to ring I was drinking scrumpy with you in mind. You have to say what happens next. If nothing, well and good. But that is said not without regret. Meanwhile, I think of you."

And received a letter at the office by return:

"Oh Ben! I think I can go on now. I say that now, but who knows? I might just need to see you, hold your hand. It may

121

sound feeble, but just knowing you are there, an ear and, dare I say, a soul?"

And more, in sprawling paragraphs, about herself, the sun and sea, the children and the sea-gulls and the ripples at low tide. Unlikely poetry from a woman whom he'd always thought to be a rare combination of earthiness and sophistication. And how hot it was. The weather pattern seemed to Ben to change dramatically somewhere between Devon and West Dorset.

Liz stood on the cliff that late July and thought of Ben and watched the sea and thought of Ben and put her hand on hot rocks and thought of Ben and thought of Ben and thought how she would describe the hot rocks and the sea to him and thought of Ben.

"I think I know the place for you," said Mrs Adderley.

"The place for me?" He was holding samples of plastic tiles which needed ordering. "This marbled blue, I think you said you liked—it's flexible—and less expensive than the Grecian range."

"I see you in a verdant place, like this, but grander, mountains, streams, a lake perhaps . . ."

"Oh really? If you could choose . . . this green for instance . . ."

"Your special landscape, fishing boats perhaps, a settlement in the shelter of the mountain . . ."

Ben held a blue tile in his hands and bent it.

"You are the place you need," said Mrs Adderley. "Each person has a place, a landscape . . ."

Ben took a white tile and placed it end to end, flush with the blue one on the table.

"And those who are in the place they need are . . . I'm sorry . . . I'm confusing you . . ."

"Oh, not at all . . . it's fascinating."

He left her feeling puzzled. Down at the Adderley's was another world like Shangri La gone wrong. But, driving back, he thought up special landscapes, tailor-made for everyone he knew.

In the office Joan waited in her red skirt, aggressively for dictation. He looked at her; Joan's special landscape would be a bumpy disused farmyard, brambled, unkempt rusty shafts and cogs of tractor pieces, rakes and ploughs, discarded under elderberry bushes.

"Sunny, isn't it?" said Ben.

"I didn't really notice."

"I see," Ben pushed his swivel chair back and crossed his legs and guessed dictation would have to wait. "What is it then?"

"Oh nothing. You dictate."

"Let's have it, Joan. What blow has life dealt you this morning?"

"It doesn't matter."

He changed his Adderley individual landscape of her; it was still the disused farmyard, still the broken farm machinery, but on a cliff edge where the land eroded and rough seas daily threw up pebbles. A beach down there you could not bathe upon.

"All right," she said, "we've got to have this ghastly tennis party. My mother's gone completely mad about it and she says . . ."

"For Christ's sake Joan; that sounds fun! You mean to say you have a tennis court?"

"Well sort of. It's the Vicar's partly. *You* can't play tennis, can you?"

"Well I used to. But, no, of course I can't."

Joan sucked the end of her Parker 51; she could be blushing. Sea pounded on the pebbles and her cliff.

"But Win can play."

"You mean your wife?" The cliff, Joan's face, had fallen, crumbled, chunks of earth dislodged, dry tussocks parting from the mass.

"She loves it. And she's very good at it. Or used to be."

"Well I suppose you'd both better come, then."

Ben leaned forward, reached the desk, his pipe, his matches, his tobacco tin. Under the map of Dorset Joan sat explosively, Parker 51 between her teeth, legs quivering as far as you could see them.

"Could this be an invitation by any chance?" he said as nicely as he could.

"You could call it that, I suppose."

"Well, if it is, we'd be delighted."

"Would you? Are you sure? What about your children?"

"What about them?"

"Wouldn't you have to bring them or something?"

"Would we? Well yes perhaps we would. What would your mother say to that?"

"Well actually she suggested it."

"Your mother sounds a nice and thoughtful person."

Joan shrugged her shoulders, bit finally through the casing of her Parker 51, and then applied her peculiar and uncomfortable landscape to the making of shorthand outlines.

Win got out her tennis racket, undid its frame and felt its strings. Ben stood in the bathroom and watched her in the garden, swinging it, a gesture he had not seen her make for years, a physical movement unconnected with domesticity.

"All right," she said, "we'll go, but I can't think why they've asked us."

He gave her money with which she bought a white divided skirt, an aertex shirt, new white socks, thick-soled gleaming Dunlop tennis shoes.

"At least it will be something to do with the children on a Saturday afternoon," she said. "That's something at any rate."

Win's landscape was a gentle rolling piece of countryside with small hedges, streams, birds singing in a rose-pink sunset deepening to magenta skies above. Moreover, she would win the game of tennis.

Liz wrote: "Oh Ben. Oh God. They are synonymous. I seem to need to see you. A letter would be something."

He wrote a letter after office hours, addressed to c/o Rosemary. In the empty typists' room he put an envelope in Joan's machine. Beside her chair the dark green metal waste-paper basket had raspberries mixed with cigarette ash and torn up carbon paper. Half-mouldy raspberries, they were, patched with grey; there were also chocolate wrappers, empty sweet bags. The keys of her typewriter were sticky.

He took a clean envelope and moved to Kath's German machine and addressed the envelope to Liz. Then he typed a note to Joan and left it folded on her desk:

"Forgot to say that you forgot to say what time on Saturday? Win needs to know and is practising hard. What a waste of raspberries; you are a wilderness. Love, BH."

Joan in the morning read this and folded it again and put it in her bag and kept it probably for ever.

Ben found more landscapes on his way home. Liz was the Mediterranean coast where you walked on rope-soled sandals with iron-barred verandahs dripping scarlet geraniums and smelt sun-tan lotion, wine and heard Flamenco music.

One morning he said to Joan: "All set? For the party?"

"Yup."

"You're always saying yup these days."

"All right then. Yes."

"So purist, aren't you, about the use of 'Good self' and 'affair' and so on. I wonder why you use such vulgarisms as yup."

"It's American, I think. I get worried that my accent is too clipped and upper class."

"Of course it is. You're stuck with it."

"I suppose I am," she looked surprised.

"But if," Ben said kindly, "if you like Americanisms, OK, baby then, let's go."

Joan laughed. She laughed hysterically even. Tears came to her eyes and he'd never seen her laugh like that; it worried him to see her use a handkerchief about a feeble joke.

ELEVEN

THERE WAS NOT a lot that anyone could say to Sally; nor did Sally want them to ; that way it made it easier for her to stay at Green Pastures. She lay on her back on the lawn in her bikini and every half hour turned over to her front. All the exposed parts of Sally became an even glowing brown, not quite mahogany, not quite oak, but like some wood that has no grain in it, some highly treated and expensive leather of rare shade. She moved her lilo round the lawn; she lay on the west side by the carnations in the morning, the north side of the lawn below the terrace in the afternoon, and in the late afternoon moved to the east side against the silver shrub border until the evening, at which time her father wheeled the drinks trolley out and put it parallel with the swinging garden seat.

It was not always sunny that second half of July, but taken as a whole second half of any July, there was more sun than rain or cloudy weather.

Sometimes she sun-bathed without her sun-glasses, so that her whole face would be the colour of her body, which Joan had to admit one evening when she went to supper there, was perfectly proportioned.

Sally washed her hair more frequently than most girls did in those days and brushed it dry as she sun-bathed; it curled either out or under at the ends depending on which way she brushed it. Joan came to envy Sally's hair. That Sally's nose was too long and her eyes not especially deep or rivetting or well set began to matter less and less when you were confronted with the whole of her. She had nice clothes too, simple summer dresses, wearing them shorter than was fashionable, but who would not, with those legs?

Joan had to tell herself continually that none of these physical attributes could make up for being permanently miserable.

126

Mrs Pridaux took Richard to one side one evening and said could he possibly take a week off work to keep Sally company. He asked at Critchells and they said yes, he could take one week now and one in August. Joan was furious; they had planned a fortnight late in August together when she had her time off from Pullers.

So Richard stayed at home and helped his father in the garden and did some studying while Sally lay on the lawn and did not want to talk to anyone. His mother said one day that he should take her car and drive Sally to the sea. They did this and they talked about their childhood on the way and about their parents, but not once about Sally's own sad circumstances. But Sally, sitting looking out at the sea from the beach at Burton Bradstock, said: "I'm not sure if I like your Joan or not."

"You don't really know her," Richard said and felt at the time it was unfair that he could not say to Sally that he'd never really liked her Johnny much.

Sally had a direct way of asking questions: "Do *you*?"

"Do I what?" said Richard.

"Do you really know her?"

"Yes of course I do. As well as anyone can know anyone. Extremely well!" He stood up on the pebble shelf.

"Oh yes," said Sally, unimpressed.

He ran down to the flatter part of the beach of gritty yellow sand and towards the waves which were high that day to the west of Portland Bill. He swam out first in breast stroke, then in crawl. They say at Burton Bradstock you can get in difficulties with the undertow. People have been known to have swum out and disappeared, unable to swim back.

A long way out, with Sally on the beach a spot of colour, white bathing-suit on green towel, Richard trod water and felt the pull of the water all around him. He considered his position; ahead the beach, Sally at twelve o'clock from him; to the right, at two o'clock, the coast-guard hut; to the left the dip in the cliff at ten o'clock. Time to swim back. He set out with slow strokes, strong slow strokes. He swum as strongly as he ever had, but at times his strength seemed equalled by whatever it was that fought to keep him away from the beach and Sally and ultimately Joan. At the peak of a wave he checked the shore; the coast-guard hut at two to the right, the dip in the cliff at ten

127

to the left. Unchanged position, Richard told himself, and went on swimming. If he used every muscle in his legs and arms to overpower the all-surrounding water, he would, he knew, get back. Use every muscle to the uttermost.

He did get back; the coast-guard hut was at two, then half past two, the dip in the cliff at ten then half past nine. Richard's blond head a dot on the blue water. He pushed himself against the undertow with every stroke, head on, head down, lungs bursting, large hands like paddles to displace salt water, driving himself on towards Sally on the shore and Joan this evening.

He stood under the cliff and rubbed his hair, water dripped from his body, still strong after all that strife, and panting heavily. Sally looked up at him and said: "You know, you're mad."

Richard, chest heaving, gazed out to sea, wet faced and said, "I know," with pride, and planned how he would tell Joan how he had swum.

And later in the car Sally said, as if to make some rapprochement, "I only asked about Joan because I know so well how easy it is to make mistakes however much you love someone."

"Did you two have a nice day?" Mrs Pridaux asked, coming out of the french windows on to the terrace before dinner.

"Yes thank you, Mum."

"Oh good. I thought you would."

Then Joan arrived, straight from the office. "I thought it would be nice for you to come, dear. I expect you're missing Richard. I understand you usually have lunch together."

"Yes we do."

"I won't keep you a minute. You stay here. I want a word with Richard in the dining-room."

Sally, Joan and Mr Pridaux sat on the terrace beside the drinks trolley and talked to cover the whispered conversation in the dining-room.

"Now listen, dear," said Mrs Pridaux. Richard stood by the table playing with a table-napkin in a silver ring. "Now listen, dear. Do leave that serviette alone. I don't want Joan to go and pry with Sally. We've kept it very easy for her so far. I'm sure Sally doesn't want to talk about things. Joan is the last person she would . . ."

"I'm sure she wouldn't, Mum. Joan wouldn't, honestly."

"I just thought I'd mention it."

"I see."

"I'd like you to tell her . . ."

"I can't, honestly . . . she won't anyway . . . I mean she's not that interested . . ."

"Well, really, Richard. Of course she's interested. She's fond of you so naturally she'll be concerned about Sally."

"All right. I'll tell her." He walked around the table a couple of times and did not go back on to the terrace. He stretched his arms and felt like running and knocked a cut-glass tumbler off the sideboard. The swim was not enough. His mother came in from the kitchen carrying a dustpan and brush. "I should have known," she said. "You children, really!"

At dinner they talked about the nationalisation of the coal mines. Sally wore a cream linen dress and said very little.

They talked about the National Health Service; they did not approve of that much more than they did of British Railways or the coal mines. People should pay for what they needed. If they worked, it could be done.

Joan said: "Supposing they aren't intelligent enough to work or they are ill?"

"Well, cripples of course my dear . . . ," said Mr Pridaux wiping his chin with a starched napkin.

"And very stupid people?" Joan said.

"Even the very stupid can be taught enough to keep them from starvation," Mrs Pridaux said.

"But if they only have stupid people to teach them?"

"Come, come, Joan. There is state education for all, for everyone these days."

"They say that in some places it's not very good."

"If people don't take advantage of the best there is," said Mrs Pridaux, "they only have themselves to thank, unfortunately for them."

Mr Pridaux looked at Sally: "Now Sal? You've been a teacher, what do you say?"

"I don't want to argue with you, Dad," said Sally getting up from the table and leaving the room. They heard her go upstairs and shut the spare-room door.

Mrs Pridaux looked at her husband. "Now you've done it,

E   129

dear." And she looked at Joan and said: "We have to be careful not to talk about anything controversial, I'm afraid."

"I thought it was just an ordinary argument," said Joan.

Mrs Pridaux smiled. "Is *any* argument ordinary?"

Richard was making faces across the table, kicking Joan beneath the table, mouthing at her. She said nothing else and tried to fold her table-napkin neatly. They had given up table-napkins at the Falconers' years ago and she was never very good at folding things.

The plates were piled and put upon the hatchway; the silver was collected and put in a jug of warm water to make the washing up easier, the napkins were put in the sideboard drawer. Mr Pridaux put the plastic apron on, took off his cardigan, put his cuff-links in a saucer and rolled up his shirt sleeves. Joan stood with a cloth in hand.

"Not that cloth, dear," said Mrs Pridaux.

Mr Pridaux sang as he washed up, the Captain's song from *HMS Pinafore*. Then he sang Trot Here and There from *Veronique* and laid each silver spoon with care upon the wooden draining board.

"You go and talk to Richard, dear," said Mrs Pridaux to Joan.

In the drawing-room Richard sat with legs stretched out on the black and white woven rug. He pushed it along the polished floor with the weight of his size ten feet. He jumped up as Joan came in and straightened the rug. "I thought it was my mother."

Joan sat down beside him on the sofa; he held her hand, but looked furtively towards the door.

Joan said: "I didn't mean to upset Sally."

It was dark and still that night when Richard cycled home with Joan across the top lane slowly, stopping in a field. He said, "I love you."

"Your parents hate me. So does Sally."

"Of course they don't."

"It doesn't matter if they do."

"They mean tremendously well."

"Most people do."

She smoked while he told her about his swim in detail, from the time he ran down the pebbles, leaving Sally on the green towel to the moment when he got back there.

130

"Sally's very strong," said Joan. "She's the sort of strong person who you feel it doesn't matter when they are unhappy. I know that's a horrible thing to say."

At half past ten Mrs Pridaux went upstairs rather slowly because she was extremely tired. That day she had gardened, helped her daily woman wash all the bedroom curtains, driven into town for market day, been to a meeting of the orphans in Dorchester and cooked a dinner for five; a very nice dinner too.

She paused outside the spare-room door and knocked. There was no reply, so she opened the door making as little noise as possible and looked in. The newly washed curtains were undrawn and moving slightly by the open window. Sally was on the bed, a sheet up to her waist, her breasts bare, Sally, curled up with her face towards the window.

Mrs Pridaux had only once seen her in this double bed with Johnny, on which occasion she had noticed that they both slept naked.

The startling things about this view of Sally were: one—her white breasts against her otherwise brown body; and two—her very dark hair spread out on Mrs Pridaux's bleached white hemstitched pillow-case. Mrs Pridaux stretched out her hand to touch the hair, but then withdrew it. Instead she drew the curtains as silently as she could and thought about the next day.

Joan was paid on Friday morning, and at coffee break she ran down the office stairs and out into West Street. She crossed the street to the Swan Hotel and turned right, up past the town hall, along the wide pavement to the new dress shop which had opened earlier that year. She passed the bookshop, passed Lloyds Bank, Westminster Bank and Barclays, passed Richard's office without looking in and came into a part of East Street where the shops were smaller, lower buildings.

There was a single dress draped on display in either window of this low-beamed shop, but these were smart dresses, for parties or for weddings. Joan was not there for them. She pushed the plate-glass door and went inside. A woman got up from a wicker stool and came towards her, hands together. "Ah Miss Falconer?"

Joan panted. "I came to buy those shorts I saw the other day."

"Ah beachwear! I remember."

"Well not really for the beach. Just for anything."

"For cycling in?"

"Not really. Can I try them on again?"

The shop was carpeted and hushed and stuffy. Miss Frayn took the shorts from a shelf and led Joan to the changing-room. At the back of the shop the cubicle was curtained off, but faced on to a builder's yard. This town had alleyways off all the main streets; you never knew what you would see from windows on to alleyways.

It was warm, enclosed and Joan could smell herself and Richard as she took her skirt off. She could hear Miss Frayn and her sister, the other Miss Frayn, in low conversation.

The shorts were scarlet with a zip in front. She'd never seen a zip in front before. Miss Frayn said the shorts were French and quite the latest thing; she'd sold a pair to Lady Carter's daughter who was off to Cannes as usual. But not red ones; Miss Falconer need not worry; these were Paris originals.

"It's OK. I'm not going to Cannes," said Joan.

"It's not everyone who can wear them quite so short," said one of the Miss Frayns.

Joan came out of the changing-room and down the shop towards the swivel mirror. Miss Frayn adjusted it. "Ahh . . . yes . . ."

One *could* wear things like this *in spite* of faulty legs. In fact, if looked at as a whole the legs weren't bad. In fact above the knee they were better than a lot of people's legs, i.e. they did not bulge. There was a cuff of linen at groin level. Above that they hugged the figure and the bottom, hugged everything between the waist and crutch. And hugged that too.

"My knickers show," said Joan and blushed.

"Hardly at all," said Miss Frayn.

"I might have to cut them off at the bottom . . ."

"Oh I hardly think so . . ."

"I mean the knickers, not the shorts."

Miss Frayn leaned against the glass counter where they kept twinsets and jerseys. The other Miss Frayn folded her arms and looked at the floor near Joan. They waited while she turned herself round several times: "I'll have them!"

132

"Something to go with them? Perhaps a sun-top?"

"No. That's all."

"We have some very dashing little halter neck numbers."

"No. Honestly thanks. That's all."

Joan's wages were five pounds a week and the shorts cost four of these. In the changing-room she opened her wage packet. This week it was £4.10s.9d. after tax and insurance.

She ran with the brown paper bag along the street and up the stairs. Mr Hodges stood outside the typists' room. "You look hot," he said.

"Oh . . . I am . . . I'm absolutely puffed . . ."

He considered her at the top of the stairs. Her landscape was quite clear today. The cliff top ran down inland to a golf course, links, a green, a putting green.

"I'm looking forward to tomorrow," he said.

"Yes, so am I . . . beginning to . . ."

Miss Frayn opened the shop door and flapped it back and forth. The other Miss Frayn fetched an atomiser they kept for just such problems and squeezed the rubber bulb a good many times.

"Hey baby!" Ben Hodges put his head around the typists' door.

"Hey what?" said Joan.

"Forget it."

"No. What did you mean?"

"Such talk brought a rare smile to your lips the other day."

"Oh did it?"

"Like I said, forget it."

Joan put paper in the typewriter and turned the knob. She said to Kath: "I don't know what he's on about these days." She giggled rather. Kath stared at her. Joan giggled.

"Golly Moses," Kath said.

"Oh Golly Moses," Joan repeated. The bursting urge to giggle started in the diaphragm. It rose like sickness and exploded into noise. You had to lean on your typewriter and choke and shake. You leaned back, laughed at the ceiling, pawed the air, the desk. You told yourself to pull yourself together. So your face was straight for seconds, then the feeling in the diaphragm arose and overtook you. And when you laughed, whether leaning forwards clutching your stomach or putting your head in

133

your hands or your hands over your mouth, your eyes were filled with tears which made the sunlight from the window dance. And you knew that it didn't matter if you could laugh like that what kind of legs or arms or hair you had, what shorts, what shoes, what skirt or blouse, what boy-friend, family or job.

TWELVE

FROM THE CHURCHYARD the whole village was spread out below you, but immediately at your feet, down there beyond the tombstones and the short mown grass, the roof of the Old Rectory and its garden spread out up the valley. Its grey tiled roof, and then you saw the copper beech turning green towards late summer. Patches of lawn, then the borders and the path, the goldfish pond, more borders. Then the hedge into the kitchen garden, the fallen raspberry cage, the bursting greenhouse. You saw the tennis court, the stream, the paddock where the ground began to rise in ridges.

Joan stood outside the church door holding the parish brown enamel teapot. She had fetched this, this gigantic teapot, from the Parish Room.

To get back to the Old Rectory you took the steps which vicars had taken for centuries before you, between the encrusted tombstones, through the little wooden wicket gate in the equally encrusted rough stone wall.

She ran down, bouncing on her plimsolls, wondering how her red shorts looked if someone saw her from a distance, narcissistic always, liking the churchyard on a summer's afternoon, the short grass, thick round base of tombstones, well worn path. And here on the dividing wall grew red and pink valerian which has a thick and herby smell, an almost animal smell which makes you stop and lift your shoe and see what you have stepped in.

Red Virginia creeper on the wall above, she came round the corner of the house, and on the big lawn at the back the biggest copper beech with sweeping low branches on which as a child you climbed and swung, under which Mrs Falconer had put the old deck chairs. The Tremletts had arrived and sat there with the Colonel, testing the fraying canvases, the shape of their bottoms visible, the canvas strained.

135

It was Mrs Falconer's day. She moved with force and shouted orders in the kitchen where the table was covered with plates of cake and scones and cucumber sandwiches. It was like old times she kept on saying and like birthday parties before the war. Mrs Northover stood at the scullery sink and had been there all day.

The Colonel had his upright canvas chair with arms. Repaired last year, this bore him well and kept him sitting comfortably, feet in polished shoes on ground. He could look down on the Tremletts. He liked Arthur Tremlett but Averil fluttered at him, oozing fluffy charm he could not stand. He did not know what to do with guests at two o'clock; you could not offer drinks. He'd had a whisky before lunch and could only get another now by deserting guests, and this was a thing he'd never do.

The grass under the copper beech, where permanently in the shade, grew thick and moist. From the kitchen the voice of Mrs Falconer echoed. It was her day and she wore a tennis dress she'd bought in 1938, pleated, reaching to her substantial knees, and floppy. It had a loose wide tie of silk just above her low bosom. It was all less than white now, but Mrs Northover had ironed it.

"But you're not playing, are you, Mummy?" Joan said.

"Oh no. Good heavens no, but I thought what fun to get it out again." It was a girlish dress from girlish times and Mrs Falconer did run about a bit and pushed grey hair out of her eyes. "We'll start directly the next people come," she said to Joan.

"OK."

The Pridaux parked the Humber in the village street and walked up to the front door between the stocks, tobacco plant and catmint. Richard pushed the front door open and stood aside to let his mother enter first.

Sally was not with them. Having decided to wash her hair, she said she'd come on later in the other car.

There were not enough deck chairs on the lawn for everyone to sit, so they stood with rackets held in frames or canvas covers, Richard in cricket trousers, his father in new white shorts and Mrs Pridaux in a beige blouse and beige linen skirt. Mrs Falconer came fast out of the kitchen door with hand extended, full of greeting, size and energy. "Well everyone knows everyone I think," she said, as sweeping in her welcome as the branches

136

of the tree swept to the ground, as hearty and unthinking as she was the day she bought the tennis dress. She was the buoyant focus of a dislocated group as the Vicar and his wife arrived.

She ushered all of them across the lawn towards the entrance to the narrow path and sent them single file towards the kitchen garden and the tennis court, a trail of people in white and beige, ducking their heads where rose briars flapped at them, dividing into two files to circle past the goldfish pond, and leaning sideways where the bramble hedge bulged out. She called from the rear: "We've worked the pairings out."

A sort of summer house beside the court. A wooden shelter, rather, stained with dark creosote years ago, with bench seats deep inside. You sat in here to watch, particularly if you were Mrs Pridaux with neat white open-work court shoes and pale nylon stockings. But, if you were Joan, you sat on the grass and watched the Vicar serve with such élan that it stretched his body violently and his hand went to his crutch each time as if his reach would wrench the tendons by which his testicles were held.

The Colonel sat on the hard bench shelter seat beside Mrs Pridaux with his chin in his hand and wished he had brought his canvas chair down here. He was silent, thinking of a possible excuse to go and fetch it. But Mrs Pridaux made conversation about the Waifs and Strays and the County Council and avoided the subject of Civil Defence.

In front of them the court, the boundary netting, white balls passing low. Averil Tremlett, who was in her forties, was partnered by the Vicar and was good. She stood forward at the net, bent at the waist, eyes darting as Mr Pridaux slammed the Vicar's service back. She never missed a possibility, but when she bounced and reached with one hand to a ball above the head, she felt the need, with the other hand, to cup a breast.

Richard was umpire, standing by the net.

The Vicar's wife could stop a ball, return a service sharply. She, being ten years younger than Averil Tremlett, was more in the brassière generation and wore one under her shark-skin tennis dress. Her partner, Mr Pridaux, said "Well done" frequently, or "A good one, very good" or "What a smasher!" He was concentrating on the game, and, if he looked at other than

E*   137

the ball, it was towards his wife in the shelter with the Colonel.

Arthur Tremlett did not play. He came in a grey flannel suit and white shirt; he smoked a small cigar and leaned against the shelter or walked between the shelter and the court. The Colonel liked him; they shared anecdotes and drank in the pub together on occasions. Arthur Tremlett had been in MI5.

Joan sat with the bottom of her red shorts on the grass and her legs bent up in front of her. She watched the bumps and rises in the grass, the way hard shots went crooked unexpectedly. From down here you could see the way mown grass is striped dark green and light green, and if you moved a little sideways, you could see the dark green stripes had changed to light and the light green stripes to dark. She wondered why the Vicar did not wear a jock strap.

At this time there was silence in the shelter. The Colonel had to speak to Mrs Pridaux and for no reason in particular he said: "A fine son you have . . ."

"We are quite pleased with him," said Mrs Pridaux.

Arthur Tremlett walked up and down the far side of the court, his cigar end pointing towards the sky. Clouds crossed this slowly, full and white and round. Once he jumped out of an aeroplane and parachuted from just such a bright blue sky down into France.

Mrs Falconer had half run up the narrow path to see if anyone else had arrived. She panted in the kitchen while Mrs Northover in her sacking apron sat on a wooden chair beside the Aga cooker, smoking and dropping ash into the bucket of anthracite.

"Your daughter well?" the Colonel said to Mrs Pridaux.

"Oh yes. She'll be here soon. It's nice to have her home."

The sound from the court was of balls bouncing softly, rackets ringing with the hitting and Richard's even voice calling out the score. He held the netting post and bent to watch low balls and called out: "Net!" Behind him, the wire netting of the boundary, behind that the paddock, bumpy soft field grass growing yellow ragwort, the ridged hill beyond.

"Of course you have Joan home all the time," said Mrs Pridaux. "That must be nice."

"It isn't nice," the Colonel said. "It's time she went away or settled down."

They watched the players pass to change ends, saw the sweat

138

on the Vicar's red forehead. The Colonel looked at Averil Tremlett's flying bosoms as she played again. They bucked and vaulted, leaped and jounced. They were no doubt quite nice when she was younger.

"I think young people make up their own minds these days," said Mrs Pridaux.

"I wish she would," the Colonel said.

"Harry and I find it keeps us young when the children are at home."

"I don't need keeping young myself," the Colonel said, "I'm perfectly happy to go down slowly without interruption."

The Vicar bounced and served. The Colonel looked at Richard. A fine son? As good as many maybe. Who knew who was fine these days?

Joan watched the Vicar serve with sweat on his shirt under his arms, his shirt untucked, his stomach skin revealed was pink and soft. At least Richard's front was full of muscle.

When Mr Hodges came she wanted him to see her lying here, chin in hands, legs stretched out behind her. She did not even want to talk to him particularly, but just for him to see her here, watching the white balls bounce on the grass and with the stream down there, the paddock over there, the copper beeches; in her setting.

Ben and Win stood in the middle of the lawn. He held Fiona by the hand and Win was carrying Amanda. Both children looked clean in pink gingham smocks which Win had made.

Mrs Falconer thought: "What a funny little family!" But she said: "What a gorgeous baby!" and stretched out her arms towards Amanda. "Will she come to me?" Amanda did not have much choice. She kicked out her new red shoes and arched her back, but Mrs Falconer held her strongly with one arm while shaking hands with Win and then with Ben. "It's so awfully nice . . . of you . . ." she called to them above Amanda's screams ". . . to come. . . . We'll go straight down," she shouted. "They've started playing."

Ben limped and Fiona sucked her thumb, and when they got to the narrow path, he had to take small slow steps, turned half sideways so that he could still hold Fiona's hand.

Mrs Falconer handed Amanda back to Win and led the way,

139

explaining how they hadn't had a tennis party for years and years, what fun it was and how she loved small children. How old was Amanda? How old was Fiona? Where would they go to school? Did they get on well together? What fun it was for sisters to have sisters. How she'd had all girls herself and never regretted it for a minute, that there was something about an all-girls family which sparked off such tremendous fun.

Then she stopped dead in the middle of the path. Win close behind her stopped as quickly. Ben bumped into Win and Fiona started crying.

"Tell you what!" said Mrs Falconer, "I completely forgot. What a fool I am! I was going to have the toys out for the children. Oh dear!"

"I'm sure the children will be all right," said Win. "Please don't bother!"

"Of course I'll bother. It *isn't* any bother. Look! *You* go down and introduce yourself and I'll take the children and your husband back up to the house."

Win looked at Ben.

"No. Tell you what," said Mrs Falconer, "on second thoughts, I've got a much better idea. No, you and I, Mrs Hodges . . . you and I . . . *we* will go down to the tennis court and then we'll send Joan up to find the toys. That's a much better idea. Now give the baby to your husband . . ."

Win passed Amanda over. Amanda grabbed Ben's glasses and these fell into the border and landed on a cushion of camomile daisies.

"I want to go with Mummy," said Fiona.

But only Win followed Mrs Falconer down through the gate and by the bramble hedge where briars snapped back at her after the passing of her hostess. Win carrying her tennis racket and her handbag and the plastic bag she kept things in for Amanda, a dummy and a sun-hat and an extra nappy. Mrs Falconer talked all the time and Win saw the three-foot shot-up lettuces, the fig tree coming through the greenhouse roof, the vine and the asparagus bed and the misshapen cucumbers. A buzz of bees and the fluttering of cabbage whites. A wasp landed on her arm. She hoped Ben would have the sense to see that neither of the children got stung.

140

Under the copper beech he sat in the Colonel's chair; Fiona was on his knee and Amanda playing with another chair, pushing it until it collapsed, having her fingers pinched and screaming. Ben looked up through the branches of the copper beech and across at the wisteria-covered house, at the purple clematis clawing over the kitchen window.

Could this be his special landscape? It would be nice to live here in decaying semi-grandeur. It would be nice to live anywhere without small children. Fiona twisted on his knee and put her arms around his neck. She looked into his eyes and put his glasses straight and kissed his cheek.

A woman came out of the kitchen door; she wore an apron, looked at him and went back in. A breeze moved the clematis, the wisteria and the branches of the copper beech. He smoothed his hair and felt a leaf land on his bald patch. Fiona took it off for him.

From time to time he could hear the score called from the tennis court or a car go up the village street. Then silence, but from up there above his head the church clock sounded twice at half past two. Amanda started crawling instead of walking, kneeling on the front of her smock, jerking across the grass. Fiona slid off his knee; the skirt of her smock stayed up, showing her bright white knickers. She pulled the skirt down, smoothed it and ran off round the tree and back to him. And round the tree and back to him. "Where is the tennis party?"

She was coming up the garden path towards him. She could not see him yet, but here it was, the very moment, told to walk towards Ben Hodges up a garden path would be an answer to a dream you would have thought.

She walked carefully, one foot in front of another, telling herself she would always remember this, and must recall each step, each daisy head bouncing as she passed, tucking her aertex shirt into the waistband of the shorts, looking at her legs, her knees, her ankles, feeling the hair at the back of her neck with one hand to make sure it was not frizzing out, that the curls were just at the neck and nowhere else, inclining her head. She folded her arms and went a little faster.

"She walks in beauty like the night," said one of Byron's poems she had learned and copied out at school. She stopped

141

and knelt beside the goldfish pond and peered between the lily leaves. And stood up and went on walking towards him.

"My heart aches and a thousand . . . ," Joan looked at the sky and up at the church clock which stood at twenty-five to three. He might just see her here beneath the pergola between the flopped delphiniums. "Like Ruth she stood amid the alien corn. . . ." If he was looking in her direction. She moved ahead, "Full of the true, the blushful hippocrene . . . ," and came on to the lawn between the lavender bushes, unopened spikes on stiff stick stalks pointing to the sky. "Hail to thee blithe spirit! Bird thou never wert!"

He was picking up Amanda, swinging her, throwing her in the air and catching her, an exercise he had discovered shocked her out of crying. He was in this navy blue blazer Joan had never seen before, grey trousers and white shirt open at the neck. And he had not seen her coming, and he had not even looked in that direction hopefully. She had walked in beauty like the night and no one noticed.

"Hello," she said.

"Hello," he said. "I find this throwing stops her crying. How's the tennis going?"

"All right."

"I like your shorts."

"Oh do you? Thank you. I have to fetch some toys."

He followed her through the kitchen door, past Mrs Northover in the scullery at the sink and through the kitchen past the food. "That's what you've got to eat," said Joan, nodding at the cakes and scones and sandwiches. Then into the stone-flagged hall and up wide stairs and into a panelled corridor and a large dark room with a low window and a window-seat.

On the way there Fiona looked up wide-eyed roundabout her, at the ceiling and the walls and pictures, but he could not hold her hand because of carrying Amanda who was struggling, and because of holding on to the oak banister to steady himself, although the stairs were shallow. Fiona had to clutch on to his blazer from behind.

In the dark room with the window-seat Joan leaned down and opened a wooden chest and raised its lid. She pulled out teddy bears and rabbits, wooden bricks and trucks. The children stood looking into it and grabbing. Fiona threw teddies, rabbits on

142

the floor until she reached the bottom of it. Amanda copied.

Joan knelt on the floor and stared at the two of them, the evidence of his union hip to hip with Win.

He stood in the low room where the honeysuckle grew up outside and poked a frond on to the window-seat and where the curtains had Winnie the Pooh and Piglet on them, where a wardrobe hung open showing Joan's green skirt, red skirt, black skirt, where stockings lay in a pile on a chair and rows of lipsticks stood against the mirror on the dressing table.

"Is this your room?"

"I use it sometimes."

Fiona found a rubber doll and held it out to Ben. Amanda tried to climb on to the bed. Ben picked her off it, threw her over his shoulder.

Joan watched them. He looked happy with his children. This was amazing; she had never known a man to be like that. Her father kept his distance with his whisky in his study and could not wait to get her off his hands.

"Shall we take something for them back into the garden?" Joan said.

"You are a funny girl."

From behind the wooden chest in a corner of the room, behind a curtain she pushed a bear on wheels, a brown bear full of sawdust which showed through a round wound in its side. "Why am I funny?"

"I've never known anyone like you."

"I am a wilderness you said once."

"Did I?"

"In a note on Wednesday." She pushed the bear across the room; it rattled on wooden wheels. Amanda seized it, pushed it, banged it against the bed. The carpet here was faded green, the boards around it stained dark, polished, scratched.

"I don't think I like being a wilderness," said Joan, and this was the nearest she could get to a declaration of eternal love.

He looked at her at breast, at waist and crutch level, at thigh and knee and ankle level. He saw her clothes and underclothes around the room, her make-up, scattered powder, hairgrips.

"I'm sorry that my room's untidy."

People, she thought, going down the stairs, smile and look at

143

you, all parts of you and make you think they like you, want you, find you most attractive, and then they don't do anything about it. Which proves that all you thought about their liking, loving you, was wrong.

People, she thought as she went back through the hall, the kitchen and the scullery and carried with her the bear on wheels for Amanda and the dolls' pram for Fiona, should not let you think they feel about you if they are not going to do anything about it.

People, she thought as she went across the lawn towards the copper beech where she put down the bear on wheels and the dolls' pram, various torn books she had under her arm, should never start a thing they aren't prepared to finish. At least you could say Richard started something which he looked like finishing. And, if he ever showed signs of giving up, she would not let him. Ever. There. So there.

Trees, she thought, and grass and children playing, making noises, throwing books and pushing prams and bears on wheels with sawdust coming from their sides, people should not look at your erogenous zones unless they one day intend to touch them.

Ben, she thought, Ben Hodges there on her father's chair, smoking, looking up through the branches, letting smoke rise from his pipe, one hand in his blazer pocket, shirt open at the neck, throat showing where his neck is soft below the line where he stops shaving.

Children, thought Ben, bloody children always getting in the way. She wanted to be held. He could have had her breasts under his hand and felt her bottom. That's all he would have done because she was too young for more. One does not, but one could have. Not fair to Win, and Joan had Richard. So Ben lit his pipe again.

Joan, thought Ben, and Win and Liz and Mrs Adderley; small curves and large soft ones, arcs and lines, elipses, creases, crescents, areas of shade, of shifting landscapes.

Sun, he thought, as the church clock struck three, sun shafting, darting down between the leaves and branches of the copper beech, catching sometimes Fiona's blond hair and sometimes Joan's brown arms as she drew on a cigarette.

She watched the smoke from her Gold Flake mingle with his

Heather Mixture and rise up through the branches. Soul meeting soul she would say if she thought there was any point in it.

Amanda pushed the bear along the lawn and bumped it on to the gravel path beside the kitchen door and screamed. Fiona wrenched the hood off the dolls' pram, also screaming, and at that moment Sally came round the side of the house in her white shirt and pleated skirt, her tennis racket over her shoulder and white cardigan over her arm.

Joan was holding Fiona's pinched finger and Ben was throwing Amanda in the air, but he stopped doing that; if anyone ever caught his eye at first sight it was Sally with her dark hair brushing on her shoulders and her skin of all one colour.

Her Adderley landscape would be the perfect snowscape or the perfect seascape. Effortless ski-ing down fresh fallen snow or paddling to the shore in gentle breast stroke. Evening ocean with rowing boat with shipped oars bobbing and the figure on the beach against the setting sun. West Indies. Caribbean. It was up to Joan to introduce them.

Here was the Old Rectory from the back, a long and low, two storied, mullioned-windowed building, soft and yellow stone from Ham Hill which is in Somerset. Here hung wisteria. Here was a garden door out of the study to the lawn. Here was the copper beech at this place in the lawn. And at the far end of the lawn; over there, the kitchen door. Inside, a long corridor ran the length of the house, flagged stones from study end to kitchen end. Upstairs the same, but an oak corridor and carpeted with a narrow strip of brown. With bedrooms leading off it. It might not merit a photograph in *Country Life* when it was sold. When offered for sale it would say: "Dorset, a Gentleman's Residence. Set in the country of the Cattistock Hunt. Six bedrooms, bathroom (room for second bathroom), three receptions, extensive gardens, tennis court. Eight miles from the sea. In need of some repair."

Here was Ben, feeling not especially different from a lot of other men as far as one could tell; with similar concerns about his mortgage and his future and his wife, his car, his personality, his wound, his not-so-far particularly brilliant career. He did not know that when he looked into a woman's eyes and said "Hello" or "How do you do?" or "How are you?", the world for them would spin off its axis, the seismograph which took the readings of their heart and hormones, oscillated with unrecorded violence, the meteorological office of their brain found observations of the state of their metabolism which, unconforming to any previous climatic pattern, made forecasts from then on conjectural.

After tea Mrs Pridaux and Mrs Falconer were playing with the children on the lawn and down the paths and round the goldfish pond; in fact all over. Fiona had never played hunt-the-thimble before, which horrified Mrs Falconer who taught that game to all her grandchildren before she taught them anything. Mrs Pridaux looked at Amanda and saw that her face was sticky, also her hands, and carried her up to the bathroom and used a Falconer face flannel with some distaste. When she came back outside Mrs Falconer said: "Of course you haven't any grandchildren yet. They are such fun."

Mrs Pridaux said she could not quite remember how many Mrs Falconer had.

"So far six," said Mrs Falconer, "but three of those are in New England. We're going to the christening of the newest one at the end of the month."

"How lovely for you," Mrs Pridaux said. "And are you taking Joan?"

"Oh no."

"So will she be staying with relations?"

"I haven't really organised that yet," said Mrs Falconer, looking hopefully at Mrs Pridaux.

"I'd offer to have her to stay myself," said Mrs Pridaux, "but what with Sally home . . . and one thing and another and . . ."

"How terribly kind of you," said Mrs Falconer, "how awfully kind. I'm sure she'd absolutely love it. And she'd be near enough to feed the cats for me."

"I don't know what our plans will be for August. Harry's thinking . . ."

"I'm sure Joan would fit in with whatever you were doing . . ."

They were by the goldfish pond. Fiona found the thimble in a Canterbury Bell. "Can I keep it?"

"No," said Mrs Falconer. "You don't keep things from other people's houses, but I'll give you one one day."

146

"Which day?"

Mrs Pridaux had to hold Amanda in her arms or spring to catch her by the smock because the goldfish pond was near. She was beginning to be glad she had not any grandchildren yet.

"That oldest child," said Mrs Falconer, "has got a squint, I think, don't you?"

Ben watched with pride Win winning, and saw that the sun above the hill beyond the court was turning pink; a mist had dulled it. There were rooks and wood pigeons in the trees and water wagtails beside the stream. He sat on the grass and Joan watched him from the other side until the Colonel ushered everyone who was not playing up to the house for drinks.

The Colonel said to Ben on the way up: "Is she any good, that girl, to you?"

"You mean Joan, sir?"

"Yes. No good, I don't suppose. I dare say useless."

"Oh no, sir; I am glad to have her working for me."

"She can spell at least; we had them all taught to spell. Even girls should spell."

He offered Ben his canvas chair and poured him gin and sat on the ground himself with his bald head level with the chair arm. "I think they can do something about it now."

"About what, sir?"

"Having girls. I think it can be prevented."

"Ah," Ben laughed. "Incredible!"

"To do with the phases of the moon."

Ben saw how the sun was now reflected in the upper windows of the house and went on laughing.

"Yes," said the Colonel, "farmers use it. They have heifer calves to order. So, if bulls can be avoided, it stands to reason that they can be scored."

They heard the players' voices getting nearer.

"I noticed both of yours were girls," the Colonel said.

"It's not a great disappointment so far," Ben said, "but our failure rate is only two out of two not four out of four."

The Colonel liked that; he laughed and rather wished he had given Ben a whisky. "I'd give up," he said, "if I were you."

They both stood up and turned into the sun. Win led, triumphant, with Sally talking to her. Joan, at the back of everyone, carrying a box of tennis balls.

Amanda Hodges slept. For the first time in her life she slept all night. And Win let Ben make love to her and made some love to him. When she got out of bed to wash herself, she went into the children's room and looked out at the mist rising over the water meadow in the moonlight. There were good moments and bad moments and you had to keep the good moments going for as long as possible to make them memorable. Then they might mitigate the bad moments.

She walked back across the passage to their own room and realised that you never think like that in bad times. Bad times were a thing to themselves unchanged by any other times.

THIRTEEN

THE FARMERS IN the pub at Axminster on market day stared at Liz in her knee length jeans and halter neck sun-top. She wore dark glasses, held a newspaper in front of her and had a half-pint glass of cider on the table.

She'd thought a lot about what to wear, bearing in mind that she must not look dressed up. This meeting might be the be-all and end-all of her life, but Ben must not guess that. This was the kind of unselfish thought which he inspired in her, she thought with pride.

Things were going on all over Axminster; the market stalls were close together in the square outside; cars parked close-packed in streets and in the small car park. Trains on the main line from London stopped at the station just to the west of the town. Children in navy blue uniform in the lunch hour from the Grammar School were let out early this last week of term while teachers wrote reports. They stopped in the market square and bought ice creams.

Ordinary things were happening which Liz, in the tradition of women in love, could not belong to.

The colour of the cider, yellow, gold or tawny: unimportant. The stares of the man behind the bar where she bought the cider: of no interest. The stained-glass window on to the market square, the copper mugs in a row: all unobserved, peripheral. But memorable in a poignant fashion. The letter she had from her mother this morning telling her an aunt had died: as nothing. The deep cut on Dominic's leg for which he had an anti-tetanus injection yesterday, also stitches: incidental.

Important were the things she wore: her espadrilles from last year's holiday in Brittany, her gold watch and bracelet which were presents from her mother. Vital: her wrists and hands, brown and narrow with long fingers, her neck, the back of which

149

was spiny with the thought of Ben. Grave: were the issues to be solved between them. Paramount: the letter he had written to arrange this meeting. Pivotal: this place in time and space. Urgent: that he would come soon.

In fact she would remember all the things in the pub, the stained glass and the copper, the fat farmers' necks and smell of dairy farming, the taste of cider. Unless it became habitual that she and Ben met here every market day and these impressions became continuous and contiguous with meeting.

She was dedicated to Ben. All of Liz was dedicated to Ben: short hair and sensitive neck, wrists, breasts, vagina, hands round cider glass. There was nothing you could name of hers which was not dedicated to Ben.

A boat which sailed out of port three weeks ago, or to be exact, three and a half weeks ago, that is to say twenty-five days —the weekend which he came to stay—might now heave into sight of land. A balloon which went up that weekend might now be losing height about to sit sedately on the ground again.

Her ankles, narrow, one twisted behind the other on the bar-stool crossbar, were twisted because of Ben. Name the parts of Liz undedicated to Ben. Impossible, unless you counted the cut finger in elastoplast, but even this she hoped he would notice and feel responsible for.

Name the parts of Liz's life undedicated to Ben. There were none. The meal she cooked for Geoff the night before was really cooked for Ben. Geoff's car in which she drove to Axminster, was aimed at Ben. The paper that she bought to read, she read for items which might interest him. Her children, if she thought of them, she thought of through his eyes, assuming he would love them as she did.

In spite of all this she firmly told herself that there was no future in it. When he came she would be calm and continent and take rejection. But she would tell him that she had always loved him. She would say she knew that he loved Win much more than Geoff loved her or she loved Geoff, that she did not want to spoil Ben's life, that, if he felt that they must not meet again, then she would agree, and they would not meet again. But she had always loved him, she would add.

Name anything that Liz had which she would not offer him. Oh life oh limb, there was nothing there to name.

Prepared to be rejected, continent and calm indeed she was, but she would just mention by the way that Geoff insulted and outraged her still with girl after girl and never gave her house-keeping on time; and sometimes not at all; how Geoff hit Dominic twice and neglected Simon; how she had no one else to turn to. Her mother, widowed and remarried, lived in Ethiopia. Ben might not know that.

Her father died when she was twelve; her mother married secondly a lecturer and went to Ethiopia. Liz was educated here and there and never all that well, but saw herself as of reflective nature, but extrovert in spite of this. But deep, she knew most people said, intense and introspective, fiery, leonine. Birth sign: Leo. So admired and good looking that people thought she could not ever feel inadequate, inferior or at a loss, unloved.

The place they drove to he had passed before. Up a track above the main road north from Axminster, a ridge with parking on an open space, some common ground where on windy weekends children flew kites or watched their fathers fly them, where the view was down towards the Marshwood Vale. They stayed in the car; he took her hand. She said, "I'm shaking." The sunshine roof was open.

"Yes, I noticed."

"Yes."

"Yes."

"Yes," said Ben. The only thing to do on such occasions was to kiss the woman quickly; a) because you wanted to, and b) because there didn't seem anything else to say until you'd done it. Then it was time to say: "You are beautiful."

She said. "It's so good to hear you say that."

"You are gorgeous."

"So are you."

"I'm very ordinary."

"Never!"

"I'm nothing special, really."

"Oh my darling!"

"You mustn't, Liz . . ."

"Mustn't what?" She pulled back from him, looking into his eyes to find out what she must not do.

The next thing to do was a) to kiss her again, b) to feel her

151

body, c) to sense that she was offering her breasts and probably much more as well.

"It's *you* we are concerned with," Ben said.

"That's sad."

"How do you mean?"

"Well . . . if it was you as well . . . I mean if *you* felt . . ."

"Don't look like that. Of course I feel . . ."

"Can I go on writing to you?"

"Yes of course."

"And see you sometimes?"

"You're seeing me now."

She got out of the car and walked away, leaving the door swinging, her back towards him between two tree trunks, a steep bank down beyond. Her hands were on her hips; her back and shoulders bony, full of varied planes of light and shade, expressive shoulder-blades which he had stroked within the last few minutes.

Standing just behind her, he said: "It's all right," and touched the shoulder-blades again. She turned and fell against him, arms around his neck. "You know I love you with all my heart. There never could be anybody else."

"It's all right. It will be all right."

"But I don't know what to do."

He stroked her hair.

"He's made me hate him."

"There!" He went on stroking.

"It would have been all right."

"I know . . ."

She leaned against him. "I'm obsessed with you, you see."

"Oh no you aren't."

"You don't like being loved?"

"Oh *yes*."

The sound of wind in leaves above them and of cars going north and south along the road; a bus which you could see flash blue and white down there. "Oh Ben!"

He looked above her head. For him, it would have been enough to loosen the cotton strip which held the halter neck and was knotted between the higher vertebrae and lower it and put his head between her breasts.

For her, she would have let him strip her if he'd made the

slightest move. She would have torn off all her clothes for him and torn off his as well.

Her recklessness may just have been contained because earlier that morning she had refrained from putting in her Dutch cap.

And Ben had wondered if it might be appropriate to stop off at a chemists. Then thought not. Then forgot.

"It's agony," said Liz.

"It shouldn't be," he said. "It's just the two of us; just for now; there's you and me and the trees and no one else. Just think . . . we might not even have had this . . ."

"It's worse because I like Win, really like her. I don't want her to go through what I've been through."

"She won't. I won't let her . . ."

"I know. You're good. I'm rotten."

"You're not. You've had a rough deal. I'll tell you something. You're one of the most marvellous women I know."

"You don't mean that."

"I most certainly do."

"It doesn't feel like that from where I'm standing; that is to say, I don't feel I am marvellous. I feel miserable."

"Now come on. Get into the car." He pulled her by the hand across the short grass. In patches there was brown earth and grass grew thin. There was a patch with charcoal and the white-edged remains of a camp fire.

He found his handkerchief, a white one from his trouser pocket, and made her blow her nose. He did the traditional and chivalrous things to her. And this was touching, but was for her edged with the thought that he might never do such things for her again.

He held her hand and pulled it on to his knee. At the same time his wrist watch came into sight. She saw him looking at it. "Oh my God, you have to go, don't you? You are my God. I really think you are. That's what's so ridiculous. That's what Lawrence told us, sex-religion, love-religion and I've got it just like any silly girl . . ."

"Look at it this way . . . ," he began to say.

"I know what I'm doing; that's the silly thing; I really know; I can stand outside myself; I know what's doing this to me. It's biological and I understand it, can analyse it, but still do it." She was crying again. Tears took the bump of her high cheekbones

153

and trickled slowly down; some dried on her face and some reached the curve of her jaw-bone, and one clung there before dropping down, as if considering whether that final fall to the shoulder-bone was wise. "And the really bloody thing," Liz sobbed, "is that this is the best way to lose you altogether. That's the bloody thing; that's the rub; that all this hysterical thing is just what nice men like you can't . . ."

"Oh Liz . . . now . . . Liz . . . "

"Oh Ben. I'm sorry."

"No. Don't be sorry."

"I'll have made you hate me . . ."

"No you won't. Just think. Now listen. Shall I come and talk to Geoff?"

"Oh God no. I couldn't bear that."

"You don't want to try and put it right with Geoff?"

"Oh no. Well yes. But it's no good. I don't know."

"Why not think about it? Honestly, love, Win and I . . ."

"Win! That makes it worse."

"Well . . . think about it." He squeezed her hand.

"Don't squeeze my hand. I'm just pathetic, aren't I?"

"You know what I think about you and that is not it."

"I think I'll kill myself. I'll leave the kids at Rosemary's . . . and . . ."

"Liz! It isn't any good that way . . . you won't. I won't let you . . . understand?"

At least, she thought, he cares that much, as he put his arms around her, pulling her towards him.

This was good, thought Ben, this stopped her crying. This stopped that. One hand on nipple, now familiar. Other hand on spine, small vertebrae. Her wet face on his chest.

"Oh my God, I love you, Ben," which earlier he would have stopped her saying.

It was either lust or comfort, either admiration or affection or a mixture of all four or any two or three of them. If asked to justify his motives he might claim any one of these. Of Ben it could be said that he was going through the motions, but bear in mind that, given a choice of motions to be going through, these were Ben's all time favourites.

It might be Liz; it might be anybody by this stage. Except that he knew exactly who it was in that part of his mind in which

154

he carried Win. And technically he was faithful to her that day and for quite a long time afterwards.

She could drive in the sun and sing for a bit with love and cry for a bit with love, and know that in a day or two the crying would predominate. It would predominate and it was such a lovely summer; she could cover pages of the paper Geoff bought from school with words of endearment and things about herself and things about the children, her thoughts of love and sex and DH Lawrence and why she felt like she did, of self-analysis. She would spread herself on paper for him as she would have spread herself on that short grass.

Win took up playing tennis regularly. But in between she cried behind dark glasses, as did Liz in another part of the south west.

Ben sat beside Win on a deck chair in his own back garden. He got up and kissed her on the spot where neck meets shoulder at right angles. His lips met flesh between her hair and the shoulder-strap of her sun-dress. "That tastes good," he said and went indoors to switch the wireless on.

"It's funny, isn't it?" said Win, heart thumping, as he moved away, "that we have never heard from Liz and Geoff again."

She went on sitting in the same position watching the children in the sand-pit. Sand was spread on the grass around it, yellow sand scattered on green. The pit itself was full of beach buckets, red tin spades, wooden spades and old plastic cups from a picnic set, a wedding present. Fiona made castles carefully in a row. Amanda came and kicked them over.

Believe, said Win to herself, believe that there is nothing and there has been nothing anywhere for Ben excepting here. And everything will be all right. Believe. He loves us; he is not unhappy; he is very loving. She looked at her watch and believed that for three minutes just for practice. Then disbelieved for four.

She went and picked Amanda out of the sand-pit by the straps of her sun-suit and dumped her on the grass. She told Fiona to stop crying and made her another row of castles in the sand. The first castle came out perfectly, round at the top, increasing to its base. The second castle crumbled, the third broke down into a heap of yellow grains.

"The sand's gone wrong," said Fiona.

"No it hasn't. You have to do it properly."

"It's silly, stupid sand."

"Shut up," Win banged a fourth castle down. She hit the bucket bottom with a wooden spade. "That's how you do it." The fourth castle was as good as the first.

She went and lay on her stomach on the grass beside Amanda. Brahms or was it Mendelssohn played inside the house. She was believing at that moment and decided to go on believing. Until she stopped, that is.

FOURTEEN

AFTER THE TENNIS party Mrs Pridaux sat with Mr Pridaux in the usual place and with the usual drinks. She was listening, you could tell, to Sally washing up.

"She'll be all right," said Mr Pridaux.

"I don't know about all right, dear, but she *is* improving."

"But she can't stay here for ever."

"She *is* your own daughter, dear."

"I am glad to hear it," Mr Pridaux raised his glass. His wife's look startled him. And he had thought she might be in a mood for jokes again.

She sipped her gin and tonic, bubbles rising, sliver of lemon slowly sinking in cut glass. "You will have your little joke, dear. One can see that you enjoyed yourself this afternoon."

"I did. I hoped you had as well."

"Well you know that that sort of thing is what I find a strain."

"I do. I know."

"But I enjoyed watching Sally play."

"I didn't do so badly either."

"No, I thought you kept going remarkably well, but it was for the young people really, wasn't it?"

Once Mrs Pridaux had played tennis. And she had even played at Wimbledon—not "nearly played at Wimbledon" like Averil Tremlett, but she had played for Nottingham Ladies in 1925. No one mentioned that this afternoon and nor was anyone supposed to. You could look at Mrs Pridaux in her late fifties and believe that she had played there. If you looked closely, that is. You could see the muscled legs, now elegant but still strong; you could see the wrists that served, now knitting; you could occasionally see quick movements; you could always see the glint of strong intention and the will to win. This strong will Sally, possibly, had inherited, but Richard in his bumbling

157

clumsy way would always get it wrong. He did have a degree of single-mindedness, but this, without the skill and subtlety, was not enough.

All the same his parents at this time considered seriously his future. And talked to Sally on this subject.

"You know the answer?" Sally said.

"To what exactly, dear?"

"To Richard's problem."

"Which problem, dear?"

"Well Joan, to put it bluntly."

"Perhaps she'll go away."

"It's not like you, Mum dear, to wait for things to go away."

"Perhaps I've changed."

"It's just as well I'm here, I sometimes think."

"You think that Richard should take Johnny's place at Mansfield Metals?"

"I think he should take Johnny's place tomorrow."

"He's very stubborn sometimes, Richard."

"Yes I know."

"And your father and I . . . we do believe that once a thing is started . . ."

"But isn't it too good a plan to miss? Richard has a sense of duty to the family, I'm sure."

"To Joan as well, though, dear."

It troubled Mrs Pridaux to see Richard studying when all the time there was a plot in hand which, if successful, would call an end to all that. It troubled her to see him paying Joan attention which, if things went the way they should perhaps, an end would be called to that as well. The trouble was, she thought, that no one was as young as once they had been, she herself included. And Sally had enough worries of her own. Young people, dear, she thought cannot be told. Although you told them. Something might, you never knew, be done with Joan.

Who danced that night at the Rugby Club Summer Hop. Joan danced that night with a boy; she jived with him in fact. She swung away from him and twirled, swung back to him and twirled again. She didn't know the music, but she bounced to it, she swung, arms stretched, she pivoted, then put her back to his and twirled with him, room going round, faces near, faces far and Richard somewhere over there, selling tickets by the door. The Great Grimstone Village Hall was full, flags of the allies in the war hung up in rows from the ceiling, fairy lights above the stage, the Sky Rovers three piece band was dressed in blue, their name in silver letters on the drum.

The boy she danced with caught her round the waist, he spun her hard, she shot away impelled by his momentum beneath the flag of the United States and the Tricolor, was caught again, was gripped, both hands were held and they danced together for a passage, pointing their toes towards each other, then flung apart again.

She hadn't danced a lot because of Richard being on the door. She'd danced with the Secretary and with some of the Committee, and this boy she had refused three times before accepting.

Whenever someone else came in and bought a ticket, Richard smiled at them and took their five shillings and the door was shut again and the flags of allied countries blew. The wind had got up since the tennis party that afternoon. At midnight Richard would pull a switch and the fairy lights would alternate from on to off and off to on, balloons would flutter from the ceiling, streamers would be thrown and there would be the gallop and the last waltz. Then the bar would close. Richard was counting money, piling half crowns and florins, shillings, sixpences, in pounds, pound notes fixed in a rubber band, and all this Richard knew would help to build the new spectators' stand.

Joan danced like she hadn't danced for ages. You had to forget that your mascara was running down your cheeks, your under-arms were damp, your suspenders showing as you twirled. And when you lost the beat you paused a moment, for a snatch of time, marked time, stamped, hopped and threw your arms around like the boy did, let them fall like he did, watched his bootlace tie swing, his slicked-back coxcomb of hair fall over his eyes and watched him flick it back again.

There was the sherry bought for her by the chairman of the Rugby Club, there was the cider she had bought herself, the cider Richard bought her and now this boy had bought her whisky and she danced. She'd never danced that well. At school she'd learnt the quickstep, waltz and slow foxtrot, but had always much preferred to do the lancers, Scottish reels and Strip-the-Willow, where you skipped across a spacious floor and moved the way you wanted to instead of being guided by a partner.

159

"You're all right," the boy said.

"Thanks."

"Another dance?"

"No thanks."

"Another drink?"

"No thanks."

"Best in the room, you are."

"Oh thanks."

"Another dance?"

"All right then."

Richard watched the flags, Joan under them, and went on counting money, smiling still. He thought it looked quite fun to jitterbug like Joan was with that boy.

Back on the floor, speed up. You never danced so fast before. At the very fastest spin, the very loudest music, muscles wrenched when reaching up, but then lean back like a rag-doll flopping, speed mixing flags above your head to one bright mass of red and white and blue.

It happened that the flag of the Rising Sun, the flag of the Japanese, was up there with the others, some slip-through from the First World War when they were on our side.

She'd stared all evening at the flags, the fairy lights, the Sky Rovers' piano, saxophone and drum, made conversation to the Chairman, made sandwiches with the wives of the Committee, and sat and drank and smoked and hated Richard for not dancing with her. And when he did dance, he left the table in her charge and took the Secretary's wife on the floor for the Military Two Step, bounced and jogged and hopped, his hair shining in the fairy lights and waved to Joan each time he passed her at the door.

It doesn't matter how much you have drunk as long as you can dance it off, Joan thought and stood there panting in a pause when someone from the stage said: "Next dance please."

"I'm sweatin'," said the boy.

She'd noticed. "I am puffed," she said.

It's not unusual to feel the room go round when you have had some sherry, cider and some whisky and to want fresh air. Outside fresh air was blowing at you, clouds scudding up above, a moon just visible from time to time and Joan, leaning against the wooden shingles of the hall where usually they held whist

160

drives, fêtes and jumble sales, breathed deeply. The music inside was blaring and she listened for the last waltz which she always had with Richard. Lights flashed through windows indicating it was nearly time.

"Is that your bloke, the blond one?" the boy asked Joan. She had her T-shirt on, her black one and her black skirt, and the two had come apart.

"Yes, sort of," Joan said, undoing her elastic belt to re-assemble what had been a smart ensemble.

"He's in there; he won't see," the boy said, catching her round the bare skin of her waist and pulling her towards him for a kiss.

Joan fastened the belt and then pushed him away. "He's very strong," she said.

"Well, scream then."

"I only said I'd *dance*," she said.

"Well, what did you come outside for, then?"

He was not bad; he tasted reasonable, of whisky and of cigarettes like she did, but she listened for the last waltz and kept her high-heeled sandals steady on the ground and did not lean towards him even slightly.

Richard wondered as he took another wife of a committee member by the hand, if he should have gone to look for Joan. He would, immediately this dance had finished. She was probably all right, and either in the lavatory or helping to wash up. The dance had been a great success; twenty pounds odd towards the cost of the new spectators' stand, not counting profits from refreshments. Joan would be glad; she would not have to stand on grass this winter when she watched him play, and get cold feet. He held the wife of this committee member fairly close, his hair against her ear because she was extremely tall.

It always seemed to Joan unfair that girls had two places to protect, well three, and boys had only one and never wanted that protected when they held you, pushed you into wooden walls when all you wanted at this moment was to lean or sit on that familiar boundary wall where you had sat as Brownie and Girl Guide, made daisy chains, passed badges in proficiency and nature study.

"Come on, then!" His hand moved up; she pushed it down;

another hand on skirt, on thigh through skirt; she pushed that down. And then another hand, but this time taking hers and holding it against his trousers. This all came, Joan thought angrily, of trying to enjoy yourself and forget this afternoon.

The throb of people dancing, footsteps, heavy, rhythmic on the boards inside, but other couples out here struggling like Joan, but willingly.

"You shouldn't dress like that, or sit like that or dance like that," the boy said, "if you don't want this."

"That's not fair." The more she struggled with his hand in order to remove her own, the more he liked it. So she bit his ear.

"Fuck you!" he said.

"No, someone else. I'm sure you'll find someone else."

"There's a name for girls like you."

He wasn't bad. As said before, he wasn't bad. The trouble was he thought he was good-looking from the way he did his hair and walked and chewed his gum and stood with hands in trouser pockets, leaned or lounged and thought he looked like Robert Mitchum probably. Joan's dream was more of men who didn't think that they were devastating; she wanted men who thought they had not much to offer her and then she'd be the one to surprise and delight them by telling them how much they had, how much she liked or loved them. She didn't want it offered to her, thrust at her like this; she didn't want to fight it; she wanted to find it, in her own time to unbutton it. Until she did, it wasn't there.

There was the car park and the wall, the road down there the other side. A name for her and the last waltz had started.

In stories, at the best bits, men cupped women's breasts; they did not push them around, tweak nipples, wobble them. They didn't seize suspenders, hitch skirts up.

"I'm practically engaged," she said.

"Oh yeah, and where's the ring?"

"It isn't formal."

"Yeah?"

"Not yet, it isn't formal."

Richard waltzed slowly, looking out dreamily beside this woman's head. She was the sort of person people had to know in Rugby Clubs and who would always make good sandwiches,

162

the sort of person he and Joan would know but not be friends with. Joan and he would be quite other, rather special. How exactly, Richard could not grasp or put a picture to, or name, but there would be a house, a grand one rather, cars, a tennis court and dinner parties, Joan in evening dress; she would have changed by then, not wanting cheap black blouses, cotton skirts and silly shoes. Her sisters from abroad would come to stay and Joan and he would make love several times a day as well as night. They might just have a dog, a horse maybe and he would go on playing rugby for the next ten years at least and cricket for much longer. And his parents would be open-mouthed in admiration at the way it worked. It might be here; it might be anywhere, in Nottingham, in Australia or here in Dorset, but they would be convinced and Joan would be convinced that life was rich and full of future. He waltzed with this woman jerkily and looked out hopefully. And saw the boy come in unhappily.

Joan vomited. She was, she reckoned, sick at least six times a year for different reasons. And between these times, she thought as she retched, there was not much to be said for living, except on very fine calm days in summer. It was cold in winter when your skirt got caught in the bicycle chain and rain got on your stockings. And even dancing which could be fun could end like this, outside and having won but not enjoyed a victory with no fruits. And Mr Hodges could not even dance; he'd never touch her, not for any reason.

And yet her mother always said it should be happy ever after now because of the Welfare State and young people knowing all there was to know, which didn't seem much to Joan who could not even drink with common sense. And there on the other hand was Mrs Pridaux saying always that no one got anything for nothing and you had to work and like it and be nice. So you got up early every morning excepting Sundays for your whole life seemingly. Or even if you stopped to have children like Mrs Hodges you became small and pale in spite of being good at tennis, or, like the Vicar's wife, got fat. And only the very rich had central heating and hot baths exactly when they wanted. And people you didn't want did want you and those you wanted didn't.

The time would come when everyone, and not just Joan would vomit, not just Joan on the wall alone throwing back into the

163

road below the mixture which cost Richard, the Chairman of the Club and the boy she danced with, necked with, snogged with, at least ten shillings. Then everyone would vomit and the lanes would flow with it; the people who had come from Bristol, welcomed by Mr Pridaux, crowding with diarrhoea and no one left alive or well enough to clean it up.

She sat on the lowest step out of the side entrance of the Village Hall, head on arms and decided that it did not matter much what happened anywhere to anyone.

FIFTEEN

MORE PEOPLE WENT to America in those days by sea than air. On the boat deck of the Queen Elizabeth which was steaming, rather which was being tugged by tugs away from the Ocean Terminal at Southampton, the Colonel and Mrs Falconer waved to Joan and Richard. Then Mrs Falconer went to the state-room and the Colonel went to one of the many bars this ocean liner had. They met at lunch, when the Colonel said: "I suppose she'll be all right."

"Who, darling?"

"Joan."

"Of course she will be. The Pridaux are so kind. I think."

"Silly idea, I thought."

"You never said."

But at lunch on an ocean liner it was the thing to do to talk to other people at the table. Such nice people. The Queen Elizabeth passed the Needles and headed towards Cherbourg; there was a minimal swell, blue sky above, fine weather forecast for the crossing. They sat on deck.

"She was invited to the Pridaux's," Mrs Falconer said.

It was also fine in Leeds for the fourth day of the fourth Test match. The Colonel had his portable radio beside him on the deck. He craned his neck to listen.

"We can't afford a wedding and all this," he gestured broadly to include the sea, the disappearing Isle of Wight and the whole of the Queen Elizabeth.

"It doesn't necessarily mean they'll get engaged," said Mrs Falconer. She watched the blue sea dip into her vision and saw that the sky was flecked with veiled white clouds. She did up the buttons of her new white cardigan. In Headingley it was Lindwall from the Kirkstall Lane End. "And in any case," said Mrs Falconer, "they'd wait, I'm sure, before they married; they are so very young."

165

"Champagne's two pounds a bottle," said the Colonel. He held the wireless on his knee and heard that Compton was on 40 and Bailey batting well. Beside him Mrs Falconer stood up, her hands in the pockets of her cardigan. "When the Robsons' youngest married, they had sparkling Moselle." She was ready to stride off and enjoy the long deck walk, the bleached white boards beneath her feet and the bright and bracing air around her. "The main thing, surely," she said before she strode away, "is that they get to know each other."

She went out on deck quite late again, inhaling sea air in the night, listening to the enormous sound and feeling the bulk on which she was a pinprick moving over the face of the dark Atlantic. Soul searching for Mrs Falconer was inevitably sporadic. At her age you could worry like mad about a thing, feel really terrible about it, and then your mind went springing on to something else. She listened to distant dance band music from below.

For every child, for every grandchild's birth, for every friend who was ill, for every funeral of parent or in-law, for every shortage of money, for war and rationing and education, you had a pang of guilt or worry, a day of it, a week of it, a stab of it. And then quite suddenly you found you were thinking of another thing.

The lights from portholes bobbled on the water.

It would be nice to have a wedding to come back to. Joan would look best in cream. Perhaps Anne's oldest girl could be a bridesmaid, Hope's oldest boy a page. There was no need to have champagne except for toasts.

They had passed Lands End at dinner time. She thought of home. It probably was time to abandon the kitchen garden altogether. With just the two of them at home, what was the point of growing all those seedy lettuces? Perhaps the Vicar would like to use that ground for growing food for his family. The Vicar had a little girl of three; she'd match Françoise, Anne's oldest; organdy might be nice, or one of those new man-made materials. And, if Moggy really was going to have kittens, this time they wouldn't have to drown them all. Perhaps Joan could take one to wherever she went to live. It was bad for she-cats not to keep at least one kitten.

Lands End at dinner time; nice people at the table, charming really. And Richard was a straight upright young man, and the Pridaux what you'd call a happy family; but sad about the daughter, though. And Mr Pridaux seemed a jokey sort of person. They'd never had a winter wedding yet, but maybe, if they did, her old musquash coat could be restyled again somehow.

One couple at the table came from Kent; their daughter lived in Boston, had four children. The other couple came from somewhere in the North of England. You'd have thought that they would cross from Liverpool, but they were very friendly. We were holding our own in the Test match, 220 for 7, from Compton, Watson and Bailey. The Colonel bought wine, Nuits St Georges. He raised his glass: "Len Hutton and the Ashes." The man from Kent said he'd had arthritis but it had been cured by cortisone injections. They drank to that. The wife of the man who had been cured of arthritis said that she had heard that a vaccine was on its way which would wipe out polio. They also drank to the signing of the armistice in Korea. "Our only enemy now," said the woman from somewhere in the North of England, "will be the common cold."

Mrs Falconer held the rail and saw the moon come up and faced the South Atlantic.

The woman from somewhere in the north of England said that last time her poodle bitch came on heat she gave it special recently-invented pills; no dogs came round at all. Her son, an engineer, was working on a vacuum cleaner which would be lighter to handle than any known make of vacuum cleaner hitherto. He was working on a machine for washing up as well. He had two television sets in his house and one long-playing gramophone. His wife who was pregnant was doing classes for painless childbirth. Their last child was born with jaundice and had all its blood changed, every last drop of it transfused, and thrived. And had Mrs Falconer heard of drip-dry cotton? Within the foreseeable future no shirts would need ironing. And her son, this woman said, sold more washing machines last year than ever before. And wasn't it good news about the by-elections? It did now seem the Conservatives were in to stay.

Mrs Falconer did not quite like to say so at the time, but she *did* believe that the Attlee Government had done an awful lot of good, although you'd never vote for them. At dinner she drank Nuits St Georges and felt quite tiddly for a time.

Rain hardly fell in Headingley at all that Test match, but that evening there was drizzle down in Little Grimstone.

"Take Joan's case up for her then, Richard." Mrs Pridaux stood inside the front door. "Mind the paint work on the stairs. I've put her in the little middle room."

There were white curtains at the window and a single bed with white counterpane; beige carpet. "I thought you'd like this room," said Mrs Pridaux. "It's just between ourselves and Sally in the spare-room."

Richard stood in the doorway, hands in pockets.

"Dinner will be in ten minutes, so you've time to unpack, Joan."

Every drawer in the mahogany chest of drawers was empty. Joan unpacked and felt obliged to fold each shirt and pair of knickers, feeling very homesick.

Dinner was at the dining-room table and was cold meat and salad. Pudding was jelly with banana in it. "And what will you children do this evening?"

"What do you think, Joan?" Richard asked.

"I haven't the faintest," Joan said. At home you didn't plan; you just did what you wanted.

"Sally and her father will be home quite late," said Mrs Pridaux.

"Oh? Where have they been?" Joan asked.

"Just gone north for a day or two."

"Oh? Is something . . . ?" Joan felt Richard kick her.

"Nothing special. Just a visit, just to collect a few things. And did your parents get off all right? I expect they'll have a lovely time."

"I have to go home sometimes to feed the cats," said Joan.

"Yes, dear, but you've done that for today."

"Time for my run, I think, Mum," Richard said.

He ran past the window in his singlet, the rain streaking off his hair in the dusk, and disappeared. From Mrs Pridaux, the sound of knitting needles and from Joan the crackle of the paper as she read the *Daily Telegraph*.

168

"You are interested in current events, then, Joan?"

"Not particularly," she turned a page and lowered the paper on to her knee, "but quite."

"I hope you'll feel at ease here, dear."

"I'm sure I will."

"Because I'm not the best of hostesses and I don't always remember what people might like. So it's best to ask."

Joan said, yes she would ask.

"You see a month is quite a long time to be visiting people."

"Yes I know."

"But then, I expect you're used to visiting, to being independent and away from home."

"Oh yes . . . I've been away a lot."

"And it will be nice for Sally, having you here for company."

"I hope it will."

"You might make friends."

"Yes, that would be nice."

"I think she's very lonely," Mrs Pridaux sighed and glanced out of the window. She held her knitting up to the lamp. Joan lit a cigarette. "I think you'll find an ashtray on the bookcase. And the little table is by the window."

Joan fetched both these things and put them just in front of her.

"And, if you want a bath, you only have to say. We'll turn the boiler up."

"It's OK. It doesn't matter."

"You mean you don't want a bath?"

"Well not tonight; it doesn't matter."

"I expect you have no shortage of hot water at the Old Rectory."

"Oh often, yes. The boiler's hopeless; it's always going out."

"They do need looking after carefully."

"Oh Daddy looks after it endlessly, but it still goes out."

"So baths are rather difficult to come by?"

"There's always the immersion heater, but he gets angry if he finds it left switched on."

"Exactly; the most expensive way of heating water."

"But I switch it on and switch it off again before he notices."

"Oh do you dear? I see."

F*   169

When Joan put down the *Daily Telegraph*, Mrs Pridaux took it, folded it into a square and put it in the cupboard under the stairs with other newspapers.

"I don't know if you want to wait up for Richard," Mrs Pridaux said.

"I don't mind," Joan said.

"He sometimes runs for hours."

"I know."

"So I should pop on upstairs if I were you. Goodnight dear."

Fully dressed she lay on the white counterpane. Then she got up and took her shoes off and saw that she had made a muddy mark on the counterpane. She folded it back, exposing the pillow and the smoothly tucked down sheet, and lay down again. There were some books in bookends on the bedside table, some Neville Shute, the *Forsyte Saga*, the *Whiteoak Chronicles*, and *The Gathering Storm* by Winston Churchill. Joan had read all the Shute, the whole of the *Forsyte Saga* and the *Whiteoak Chronicles*, so picked up *The Gathering Storm* and put it on the pillow, put her head down beside it and traced patterns on the linen frill with a finger faintly stained with raspberry juice and nicotine.

She heard the car, the voice of Mr Pridaux and the voice of Sally. And later she heard Richard go into his room. But lay there, having now turned out the light.

Sally Wintersgill, née Pridaux; born 1928 in her parents' semi-detached house on the outskirts of Mansfield, Nottinghamshire. Her father was building up the business at the time. The two crates of wire nippers taken out by goods train in 1922 had built to four, the four were building into eight. If Sally had been born a few years later, she would first have seen the light of day in a detached house on the Derby Road, which is where Richard was born.

Sally Pridaux, because her father sent sixteen crates of wire nippers out each week by the time she was five, went to private school, and when she was eleven took an examination for Nottingham Girls High School. From here girls go to University, a high proportion, but Sally's parents having been advised that she was second-rank intelligence, she went to Teacher Training

College in 1946. She qualified in 1948, and taught in Primary Schools. She married Johnny Wintersgill in 1950.

He was the son of another businessman who had boomed in printing school text books and was booming even more since the 1944 Education Act, and lived in a slightly larger detached house in the Derby Road. The Pridaux and the Wintersgills played golf together and bridge together and went on holiday to Scotland all together. Johnny Wintersgill was the second son. The Pridaux liked the older brother, Nigel, best, but Johnny Wintersgill, on growing up, learned how to talk to girls, which Nigel never had. A dull fat boy with glasses called Johnny Wintersgill, who had never been good at anything and never popular, began to dress well, dance well and have his hair cut well. He'd had to learn to please and charm because he'd never been much good at anything and still was rather fat.

The knack once learned was never lost. Sally, who was not good looking, was blossoming at the time, shaping up and buying clothes to suit her previously gawky looks and becoming good at things like tennis, bridge and parties. Like Ben, Johnny Wintersgill was first smitten with Sally at a tennis party.

People said she was worth twice of him. Everybody in their large circle of Nottingham and Mansfield acquaintances said that. Johnny could not believe his luck. Here she was with beauty not skin deep and an aura which came with her of patience, solidity and dependability. At parties among young marrieds in 1950, '51 and 1952, he would leave her side and talk to fluffy pretty girls but know that he had Sally. And his career was changed; improved in fact; instead of being the second son in Wintersgill & Son, he headed for the board of Mansfield Metals.

They had a cottage outside Nottingham, bought jointly by the Pridaux and the Wintersgills, investment to be repaid by Johnny's salary from Mansfield Metals and from Sally's teacher's salary. They went their different ways each morning, coming home to a near-idyllic situation. Sally had, exactly as her mother always said, warmth and common sense, good legs, nice hair and nice clothes and an enviable young husband.

She was warned; she said to Mrs Pridaux: "Yes I know, but I can cope with that. It's all quite harmless what he does with other girls." It was harmless that he kissed his secretary, took

171

her out to dinner when Sally was away or busy marking books in the evening. It was harmless that he put his arms round fluffy blondes at parties. Sally did not like it, but she got used to it. Mature for her age, she knew he loved her best. She loved him very much, practically adored him, spoiled him. Their sex life was excellent and adventurous. They did not have a copy of *The Way to Sex Technique*; nor did they need one. One day she wanted to stop working and have his babies, quite a few of them preferably.

Her mother said: "You have your babies, but who's going to keep an eye on Johnny?"

"That's a thought," said Sally.

"You be firm," said Mrs Pridaux.

Johnny Wintersgill, working his way towards the board of Mansfield Metals, became Assistant Marketing Manager, one step from director at the age of twenty-five. The Managing Director sent him on a marketing course in London. But not alone, but with his secretary. He spent more time in bed with her at the Cumberland Hotel than he did at the marketing course. And Sally, arriving earlier than expected on the Friday evening, did not exactly discover them in flagrante delicto, but saw the secretary in the foyer, hurrying out into the lower part of Edgware Road and found a gipsy ear-ring on the pillow of the double bed.

She then was firm; hysterical but firm. Some reconciliation was achieved; he wept, she wept; he tried to make love to her, but on the same bed, stupidly, in the Cumberland Hotel within two hours of his previous love-making, and she refused him. His smooth body, as tempting to her as raspberries and cream were to Joan, and as Ben's body was to Liz and quite a few other people, Sally pushed away. She did not want to be made love to; she wanted to beat and pummel, slaughter him, impale him, not to be impaled herself. He slammed out of the room without his matching set of pigskin suitcases.

Sally, in her well-made petticoat that fitted neatly over her white bra, and in her straight-seamed nylon stockings, lay face down on the Cumberland Hotel bed all that night, crying from time to time and definitely in torment.

Once as a child she was sent up on a Friday evening to her room as a punishment for not eating cabbage. Mrs Pridaux's

172

steely glint met Sally's and she sent her upstairs. Mr Pridaux said after three hours: "Do you think we should take her something?" "No," said Mrs Pridaux. After six hours, Mrs Pridaux said he could go and see if Sally was all right. Her door was locked. "Do you think she is all right?" he asked. "Perfectly," said Mrs Pridaux. Early next morning they heard Sally come down from her attic room, go to the lavatory, fetch a tooth mug full of water from the bathroom and go upstairs again, where she stayed all Saturday, except for visits to the lavatory. She came down for breakfast on Monday just in time to go to school.

Which is the only available clue most people have about her. She survived the same amount of time alone from Friday until Monday at the Cumberland Hotel. Then she went home, told Johnny to get out and put the cottage on the market. She worked for half a term at school, and, having seen her replacement teacher safely in, went home to mother.

Joan heard them in the passage: Sally, Richard, Mr and Mrs Pridaux, whispering; then she heard them close their bedroom doors.

In Richard's room at midnight:—the piles of law books on the table by the window, his bed, his bookcase, and Richard himself in pyjamas standing just inside his door. His light was out. His hand hovered near the handle of the door. It was loose and as you turned it, often rattled. But if you took it slowly, gripped it with firm, gentle pressure, stood close to it and muffled it with your body and pyjamas, you could make it turn without a single sound.

Mr Pridaux tied the cord of his pyjamas and said how nice it was to be home again. The sale of Sally's cottage had gone well. Mrs Pridaux sighed.

In the open doorway of his room Richard considered the space of floor he had to cross. A fitted carpet, but with here and there a loose board underneath. He would go on all fours, testing first with hand to find a firm place for his feet.

"Funny child," said Mrs Pridaux.

"Sally?"

"No, Joan."

"And have you talked to Richard yet?"

173

"No dear. Have you?"

Under spread fingers Richard felt the dipping of a board. He moved his hand six inches to the right and felt again. Firm ground here six or so feet out from his bedroom door.

"It may be all too late," said Mrs Pridaux, "but since you say that Johnny's given in his notice . . ."

Hand by hand and foot by foot, Richard edged in the almost-dark along the passage, past the bathroom, then past his parents' room where he froze in mid-pace, one hand raised, for a count of ten because he heard their voices.

"In which case . . ." Mr Pridaux said.

This was the way to go, one hand forward, finger test, then, if no creaking from that board, you put the other hand and then the other foot and then the other. Quiet as a panther, inches from Joan's door. In the jungle there were sticks to crack if just an ounce of weight was put on them.

"In which case we can only hope," said Mrs Pridaux.

His hand was on Joan's door, the handle of it.

"Hope for what?"

Dim room, white curtains, shape on bed. He turned the handle, moved the door, supporting it he closed it with no squeak, no bump.

"That Richard will agree . . ."

Joan sat up; her silhouette against the window. Richard on the floor knelt up and held aloft one hand to silence her. He was here; he'd made it, in the dark and soundlessly. "It was tricky," he said softly, reaching out to her, "but I managed it."

For Sally the bumping on the floor interrupted her I'm-not-missing-Johnny exercise, which consisted of deep breathing by the window.

Mr Pridaux slept; but Mrs Pridaux did not; she knew always what was going on in every corner of her house; she lay on her back and thought how thoughtless were the young and wished that Richard was as light-footed at all times of day.

The Pridaux had breakfast at half past eight on Sundays, with white napkins, clean for Sunday, boiled eggs and toast in front of each place and kissed each other goodmorning.

In the end Joan worked out that if you were a little bit late you could avoid the kissing ceremony, rather the not-being-kissed in her case.

On working days you had your breakfast early. Mrs Pridaux got up specially to give it to you and to Richard, and you sat on either side of the table staring at each other.

SIXTEEN

She said to Ben: "They hate me there."

"I can't imagine why."

"They think I'm decadent and dissolute."

"Which you quite like."

"What do you mean?"

"I've got you wrong again then, Joan; I thought you liked that picture of yourself."

"I don't care what they think of me."

"In that case everyone is happy."

People had August Bank Holiday the first weekend of August in those days, and Joan went into work on Tuesday.

"Dear Mrs Adderley," he looked out of the window, "Planning permission was last week granted for your . . ."

"What?"

"Why what?"

"I'm waiting."

"Sorry. Miles away. Planning permission for your projected extension."

"An extension is projected surely anyway. Anything which is extended is projected."

"But not everything which is projected is extended. A projectile is thrown out and an extension is put out, extended. And anyway I meant projected in the sense of planned."

"Why not say planned then?"

Ben sighed. "Shall we go on?"

"Yes. I'm sorry. I broke my resolution."

"What resolution?"

"About correcting you."

"I'm amazed that you should have a resolution."

She gazed at the page and waited. Ben went on: "In which

176

case I shall be instructing Messrs Osmond Brothers to commence the work as soon as possible on the lines of their estimate of which you have a copy. I look forward to working on this matter. Yours faithfully. . . ."

"You usually put yours sincerely to Mrs Adderley."

"All right, Joan." He lit his pipe. "All right!" He looked up at the ceiling. He sat up straight and craned his neck towards the window; there was no one opposite in any of the windows of the Swan. He leaned back and looked at Joan. She wore her green skirt, yellow T-shirt and her tight black belt. "Have you done something to your hair?"

She looked up, eyes full of tears.

"Oh no!" said Ben.

"Oh no what?"

"Oh no, you're crying."

"No, I'm not."

"All right. Have it your own way. You're not crying."

"You're usually very nice."

"Now listen, Joan. Are you ill?"

"No."

"Well, do you want to go home?"

"No."

"Well, do you want . . . well . . . what *do* you want?"

"I don't know."

There was nothing he could do from this side of his desk. A girl on a chair in the middle of the blank wall of his office with a map above her head. A girl with crossed knees and a short-hand notebook, tears smudging inky outlines.

"Now listen, Joan; I think you should go home; do you understand?"

"I haven't any home to go to."

"What a lot of nonsense." He stood beside her. She did not put her head in her hands and weep. If she had bent down like that, he could have put a fatherly hand on her shoulder. But she just sat and let the tears run down her face and every now and then she wiped her face with her hand and her hand on her skirt. He would have to find the handkerchief he'd offered Liz last week. He passed it to Joan who took it and held it to her nose. Then he squatted beside her so that his head was level with hers and said: "Come on, now. If that's not crying

I'm the King of Ethiopia. If you're going to cry, cry properly, sob or howl or something."

She gazed at him, suspicion behind the tears, like a small animal looking out of the burrow to see if all was clear, like Amanda wondering if anyone was looking when she picked the flowers she had been smacked for touching.

"You've got the Pridaux house. I'm sure it's really nice there."

"It's horrible." She sobbed as he'd suggested, shaking shoulders, holding his handkerchief in front of her face. "They all keep whispering," said Joan. "There's secrets and it's horrible."

He took her hand: "For Christ's sake Joan . . . this is a Monday morning—a time to feel gloomy I know, but not a time to weep."

"It's not. It's Tuesday and it's not because of that."

"What is it then?"

"It's what you said."

"What did I say?"

"You said about the picture of myself I liked . . ."

"Well, don't you?"

"I don't know."

"Oh God, Joan!"

"Why Oh God?"

"Stand up and blow your nose." He pulled her to her feet.

"I'm sorry if I made you crouch."

"That's not the point. I don't like to see you crying."

"It must have hurt to crouch."

He took the handkerchief and dabbed her face for her, one arm round her. "Come on, now."

A new pair of breasts against him once again, her hair against his cheek, and over her head and through the window and across the road, the White Swan window opened and the maid in the orange overall leaned out and let the sun shine on her cleavage.

He could have said: "Now look, Joan," and have given her a lecture; a lecture on the way that people want to look, to be seen to be in order to be liked, to behave the way that will be popular. He could have told her that he for years had tried to be a person people liked. He could have told her just how stunning she would be if she behaved as if she wanted people to be stunned by her.

178

And she could have said to him that the trouble was that she didn't want him to think of her as decadent and dissolute and without resolution. That is, if decadent and dissolute people and people lacking resolution were the kind of people that he did not like. She only wanted him to think of her as marvellous in every way.

Instead she took his handkerchief and went away. She typed a letter in the lunch hour and left it on his desk:

"There's raspberries and raspberries still left. And, if you come and pick them, I go there after work to feed the cats. Yours sincerely, Joan."

"I start these letters anonymously and they are not signed. But nothing in them of the poison pen. The loving pen, the most adoring pen. You're good to read them, if you do.

"The sun rose and I was on the cliff. A boat down there; me knowing ours will not, cannot come in. There's nothing here which does not remind me of you; sometimes I wish you hadn't been here; that this summer had not happened. I sit under the cliffs and write. The sea, when I carry Simon down to it, breaks its ripples between my toes. Each part of me is yours. Geoff is strangely coming home on time—and just when I want to be alone or with no one but the obvious choice. It's enough to know you're there—somewhere in that wide street in that top office you told me about, letting your light shine on drawings and the people blessed by being in your life, and going down those stairs and into that car.

"Here the sun strikes the sea and makes it hard blue. The heat is almost painful and the children burnt. The shimmer as the boat sails out, the scorch . . ."

Such heat, thought Ben, not here but there, although in the August of that year it did get warmer. But a lot of time was being spent indoors at Ben's house these days watching television.

People were not so bothered about the preservation of nature in those days and when Joan sat in the lilac tree at the end of the

179

Old Rectory drive, she stubbed her cigarettes out on the trunk and tore off twigs to make the sitting place more comfortable. She'd sat here often in her life, in the fork which had grown since first she sat there. She had grown, but now she'd stopped growing and the fork went on enlarging, fatter, rounder, more accommodating.

From here you could see without being seen. You could see up the road which bent past the church and continued up to Hightown. Or down the road towards the pub and shop where all cars came from town.

It was six o'clock on Tuesday; then it was six o'clock on Wednesday and so on all the week. But Friday was the time to pin your hopes on. He'd been to Mrs Adderley's that afternoon. Most days Joan waited until seven, then bicycled fast to Green Pastures to be in time for dinner. But today she'd wait until seven fifteen.

She waited in her green skirt and her red skirt and her yellow skirt, her black skirt, all hitched up round her thighs and let her legs swing down. The only sign of presence in the lilac tree for passers-by was the occasional plume of Gold Flake smoke which rose out of its top between the dead head blossoms. And once the Vicar stopped and sniffed and went on past up the drive towards the tennis court. And once the Vicar's wife, once Mrs Northover, once the gardener on his Wednesday.

One day she leaned along the branch and pulled at leaves to open up the uphill view. One day she leaned along another branch and pulled off leaves and let them scatter on the drive to open up the level view towards the village.

The only hitch, apart from the hitch she gave her skirts, was that the cats came up there with her, the big old ginger, the tabby and the pregnant Moggy; they slung themselves along neighbouring branches, purring, scratching, rubbing themselves against her legs and arms and face, shaking their ears with canker in them, which rattled on these calm and windless days.

He said this morning: "Raspberries still in season?" and she, trembling at the knees said, "Yes, I think so", taking outlines in wild confusion after that.

She would hear his car whichever way it came. And at the sound, and having checked the sight through torn-off leaves, she would leave the fork in the lilac tree, swing one leg over, swing to the ground, and fast. It had been practised. And her bike was just outside the front gate, not for quick get-away or anything like that, but to confirm her presence.

Here she waited while over at Green Pastures Mrs Pridaux cooked the dinner, Richard somewhere else was playing cricket, Mr Pridaux was in Dorchester with Sally. Here was Joan, astride the fork with a cat to right and a cat to left and another cat just above her head. Not knowing if within five, ten or fifteen minutes her life would be transformed, her young heart filled with joy or disappointment, her future changed, her fears confirmed, her hopes fulfilled or dashed, her small corner of the earth made heaven or hell, her self-love encouraged or her self-hate likewise. Not knowing whether angels would blow trumpets in the sky or throw down thunderbolts.

And here she was, five minutes later, standing, looking down the road at where the Hillman drove, not having stopped, but having driven down and past.

The car came down the hill; it slowed outside the gate; his head turned and he peered up at the windows of the house. Joan jumped and stood outside the driveway in the road; he must have seen her, but he'd passed by then. But then he slowed again down by the junction just beyond the pub, but that would be to see if the other road was clear. He did stop in a way; not properly, however.

She stood by the gateway, heard the church clock strike the hour of seven, looked at the face of the clock, black with gilt Roman figures, looked up the hill, remembered how the sky was, broken cloud, that the temperature felt like a level seventy Fahrenheit, that the tarmac on the road was not really of an even texture but of several different shades of grey and white and blue, that the orchard opposite had Worcester apples on the branches of the trees and these would soon be ripe, that there were magpies there, that magpies' wings were black and white, but when you watched one carefully the black was struck with rainbow streaks like oil. He would have stopped and waited if he'd really wanted to. Face that.

So how did you get them? What did you have to say or do? Which way to sit? How should you dimple, weave a spell, make eyes at, flirt, inflame, seduce, lead on or tantalise? How sickening, how painful, how humiliating. Who said good looks would

181

win the day? Well no one actually, but Mrs Pridaux said that they would not. These questions and many more flew round Joan's brain as she let her bicycle free-wheel down towards the junction, and, as she turned to take the lane to Little Grimstone and Green Pastures and stood on her pedals when she reached the hill and leaned forwards over handle-bars along the top.

She would go away most definitely. She would walk the streets like any prostitute, make a life for herself elsewhere, be famous, infamous, be anything so that one day Ben Hodges, looking in the paper would see the face and say: "My God that looks like Joan!"

A shallow slope to start with from the top, free-wheeling, hearing the three-speed ticking and the pressing of the tyres on tarmac.

She'd make her name—Joan Falconer—a headline, and, if that was not enough, she'd make it headlines twice, three times until he saw it, looked up and said: "My God that could be Joan!"

The pressing of the tyres and the ticking of the three-speed, crickets in the bank and distantly a rabbit squealing. Fields on either side seen through gateways as you passed still gliding slowly, feet on pedals staying in the same position, balance perfect, skirt tucked up, warm air on knees and ankles, arms and face.

Somewhere in time he'd look up in his self-designed dining-room at breakfast time and see the face and give the name, put down his toast and marmalade, reach for his pipe, but first he'd wipe his mouth and say: "My God that must be Joan!"

Fields passing, some with standing corn, and clover heads on banks, plantains, thistles, foxgloves; the banks got lower here, your head above them, gliding. White road here.

Or sitting on a beach or in a train or bus or in a café, in a pub, he'd lift the paper, take his pipe out of his mouth, run his hand over his even balder patch and say to himself or anyone else that was around: "My God that's Joan, that is."

Here was the final slope down to Green Pastures in its patch of young trees, mostly flowering in the spring, but now with leaves of darkish green. The white-barred bridge, the beech hedge, the tiled roof.

How did you learn to wait, thought Win. How did you learn to keep from screaming, to move about the house and garden, bathe children, fold their clothes and draw thin curtains over summer evenings and go downstairs? And switch the television on?

"How do you do?" said Mrs Falconer to everyone at the christening of her youngest grandchild in New England. She towered above the people in the room, tall English woman wearing English silk dress and a large straw hat, sweat on her face in the hot New England summer.

SEVENTEEN

OR WAS IT your legs, your hips, your bad breath possibly? Your face, your hair, your way of speech? Because you were not like models in *Vogue*, in *Harper's* or in *Queen*, you were imperfect, soiled and had fat wrists? And Richard, having no one to compare you with, chose you because he knew no better.

Hair on the upper lip? Short neck? Bad temper? Generally inadequate?

Supposing Richard saw all this, thought better as the scales fell from his eyes.

She refused the ring. She'd always said that getting engaged was pointless. You were either married or not married. And if you said you would be married and then changed your mind, then you were not married after all. Formality, she said, like Pridaux breakfasts, lunches, dinners, was ridiculous. People should eat when they wanted to, go out when they wanted to, come in exactly when they felt like it, go to bed and only get up early if they had to go to work and get money to buy food with. People, she said, made love if they felt the urge. And, if they didn't feel the urge, they didn't make it. And, if one felt the urge and the other didn't, then what rotten luck for one of them.

Weddings were pointless, Joan said. If there was an easier, cheaper way of doing it, like going to the Registry Office first thing one morning, then that was the way to do it. No champagne, no white, no bridesmaids.

"Oh, but Joan, darling!" said Mrs Falconer, back from the States on the day England won the fifth Test match and regained the Ashes they had lost in 1933. "Oh but really!"

"All right then, but it's against my principles."

Cheques as wedding presents came in handy. But formality and ritual, three-tiered cakes and veils and invitations all were boring. Music was all right. "Well, OK then, Jesu Joy of Man's Desiring and Dear Lord and Father of Mankind, but nothing else."

"Not even Love Divine?"

"No flowers in church."

"Now darling that's just silly!"

"It would be silly to order flowers and then to have to send them back if I changed my mind at the last minute."

Richard stood in the Colonel's study; he did believe that he would get a whisky now, unprecedented. The Colonel said: "Sit down . . . er . . . Richard. I know what you have come to say and you know what you've come to say and my answer's yes, as if I had any say in the matter anyway. Have a whisky."

"I say, sir, thanks sir."

"You can say it if you like, but if you'd rather take it as said . . . I'm easy. I know the money side of it and you've got more than I have."

"Oh I don't know, sir, really."

"Well you will have. Hang on to it is my advice."

Richard had, in fact, prepared a longish speech with some fine phrasing in it; he had notes of it on the back of an envelope in his trouser pocket. Through the study window he could see Joan on the lawn on her back under the copper beech, wearing dark glasses.

The Colonel said. "So you're changing your career?"

"It would seem so, sir."

"That might be disappointing for you."

"Rather," Richard said.

"Good practice," said the Colonel.

"What for?"

"For being disappointed."

Richard laughed nervously and jerkily. Out there Joan was eating chocolate.

Mrs Falconer said: "First weekend in October. But darling that's always Harvest Festival."

"That solves the flower problem. Marrows, wheatsheaves and tomatoes would be best in any case, and the bridesmaids can wear rust-coloured things to go with all that and carry apples in

185

baskets. It will suggest fecundity, not that I propose fertility, nor am I pregnant."

"I'm afraid that people think you may be . . . all this rush."

"Then I shall prove them wrong by not having any children ever."

"Well, Joan, that's quite some news! I shall miss you. Nottingham? Congratulations."

Who said that? Don't look at him. Eyes down and say: "Thanks," a trifle gruffly and then . . . "well . . . cheerio."

"You always said you'd go away."

"I reckon if a bomb dropped there it'd drop. We'll know no more."

"You'll never know no more."

Eyes down. Don't look at him.

"Oh Joan!"

She'd call her first son Benjamin.

"I've heard from Liz at last."

"Oh really?" Ben cleared his throat, "oh really? Is she well?"

"She's leaving Geoff. She's left, in fact."

"My God!"

"She thought we'd like to know."

"No dear, I don't think Joan would like a guard of honour from the Civil Defence."

"A funny girl."

"Yes dear."

"They will be all right I dare say. He knows he's starting from the bottom and he'll have to make what he can of it."

"Yes dear, he knows."

"Where has she gone?"

"To Ethiopia. To her mother."

"And the children?"

"With her, yes of course."

"It's hot here. The sun strikes on the rocks. The sky a livid blue. We drive from Addis in my step-father's Land Rover. A mirage. I still think. Oh Ben. Oh Ben!"

186

People did not have pubic hair in those days, but Sally did, a lot of it, which Ben discovered on the night of Joan and Richard's wedding. While Richard and Joan in a three-star Trust House Hotel in the New Forest did what they had done some hundreds of times before, but in comparative luxury this time, Ben took Sally upstairs to a room in the White Swan while the party was still going on downstairs. This was the room he looked at from his office almost every day. They were both fairly drunk. They took their clothes off and plunged on to the bed.

"You are one of the most marvellous women I've ever known," he said afterwards.

"You're not so bad yourself."

"You seem to be so cool, composed, and yet in bed, I've never known the like."

"You're gorgeous," Sally said, stroking his stomach and examining his wound.

"I fell for you on the tennis court."

"I was in a bad way then."

"And now?"

"The same, but this is fun. No strings. That's what I've decided from now on."

The wound was just behind the pelvic bone; provided your fist was fairly small you could put it inside the indentation. "Am I hurting you?"

"I like it."

She stroked his thigh, his knees, his shins. He sat up and said her long back, as she curved it over him, was the most beautiful back he had ever seen.

Joan had not asked him to the wedding, so her mother must have. Joan did not bother much who came. She bothered about her trousseau and, in the end, about her wedding dress. As well as the cheques, she liked the presents and was puzzled when one came from Ben and Win because she did not know they would be guests. It was a cheese dish chosen by Win in a hurry, with a chromium knife. Joan never used it but kept it always. She stopped work a month before the wedding to get organised and had a nice time sitting in the garden reading in the late summer, then in the early autumn, eating apples and writing thank-you letters.

187

Mrs Falconer and Mrs Pridaux, Sally and Hope, who came down with her children for some weeks, did all the work. The Colonel paid. And many people in the district bought new clothes for the occasion.

The bride and groom would come down through the wicket gate on to the lawn. The marquee would spread beyond the house; beside it the copper beeches were quite green by that late time of year.

It was warm enough for Joan to sit on the sunny end of the lawn where the shadow of the hill had not yet reached and write some days before the wedding:

"Dear Mr and Mrs Hodges. Thank you very much indeed for the lovely cheese dish and the knife; it will be very useful. And is pretty. We have had lots of lovely presents . . ."

She stopped and chewed the fountain pen of which there was not much left.

The plan was that they would come down the hill between the tombstones on the side path and through the wicket gate, and with luck at the bottom they would still hear the wedding march behind them as the guests filed out.

"There is just so much to do for getting married. I wonder if I would have done it if I'd known. . . ."

She wrote this last sentence in most of her thank you letters and thought it rather funny. Sometimes she put an exclamation mark after it, but not always.

They would stand just inside the marquee with bridesmaids, pages, the Pridaux and the Falconers, and people would file in and shake them by the hand. The cake would be in the middle of a long trestle table the far side of the tent; the caterers would be from Dorchester. Three hundred people were expected.

Then there would be the church bells ringing; the bridegroom pays for these; they practised beforehand through late September afternoons and evenings. The bells would start at one and ring for an hour before the ceremony. There would have to be beer, for which the bridegroom pays, or cider for the bell-ringers in between that first burst and the final coming out of church,

188

triumphant ringing which might drown the Mendelssohn.

She would walk triumphant down the aisle to that, she finally agreed. And with so many people watching, with three hundred pairs of eyes to witness that, three hundred presents—well, one hundred and fifty, if you reckon most guests come in pairs—all those new clothes, all that time and trouble, all that music, food and drink and noise, there was a lot invested in the contract.

The bridegroom also pays for the choirboys and some of the wedding cars, but Richard would get off lightly because of the walk down from the church and through the wicket gate. The bridegroom pays for the bridesmaid's presents, necklaces and for a tiepin for the page. The drinks are on the bride's father, the food the bride's mother. But the bridegroom pays for everything for ever after, after that.

Richard bounded up the main path beside his best man, taking two steps at a time. Seeming eager, as he must, because it was his idea to start with probably.

"How sweet, how young, how awfully suitable," guests were heard to say.

When Joan stayed at the Pridaux's she would be kissed at breakfast now.

Four days to go and the marquee had arrived. She went on writing thank-you letters as the sun went down behind the hill; she moved her writing place across the lawn towards the house, her rug, dark glasses, chocolate, apples. She added to the letter: "I'm very busy getting ready; it will be fun I hope. It probably is a good thing on the whole." She thought that quite a sporting thing to say.

The evening sun could not now shine on to the mullioned windows because the marquee was going up in between. Joan sat in the shade.

Eve brought her a huge cookery book with pictures, from America. It was full of recipes for making things with sweet corn, which was in those days not to be found in many shops in England.

Sally gave her a bottle of expensive scent and dozens of pairs of nylon stockings, with a note which said: "It's rotten luck just to get presents for a house. Be happy."

Sally stood outside the church door porch. She wore a small red hat like an army cap and a navy blue coat and skirt, and

Ben beside her by coincidence. In bed that night he said to her.
"A happy couple?"

"Us?"

"No, them.".

She said: "Did *you* know any cause or just impediment?"

"Oh plenty, yes. Did you?"

"She didn't want to go away alone I think," said Sally.

Win was glad she did not go to the wedding because Amanda's temperature went up to 103; the doctor came for the second time that Saturday; it was measles. Win was too worried about Amanda even to think what Ben might be doing, but he rang twice; he even offered to come home and take over while she went to the after-wedding party at the Swan. She said: "For heavens sake I'd be too worried; let's one of us enjoy ourselves." And only when Amanda came out in a sweat at half past ten did Win wonder why she had said that. She turned the television on. Close-down was late on Saturdays even in those days. Not that there is the slightest suggestion in Win's case that the television set made up for anything.

Downstairs in the Swan the older Falconers and the Pridaux were putting on their coats. The young, as they called them, could dance all night. Self-consciously Mrs Falconer kissed Mrs Pridaux's cheek because they were related now.

Upstairs in this room which had been booked for a Pridaux cousin who failed to turn up at the wedding, Ben made love to Sally. But first he'd danced with her. He saw Joan's sisters and their husbands. Ben looked at Eve and Anne and Hope and decided they were too like Joan to be danced with; their landscapes had been organised, likewise their looks; the effect was overpowering. They knew it but Joan did not yet. A pity no one told her.

By that time she and Richard lay apart, stretched out, asleep.